I Ain't Got No Home
in This World Anymore

First Montag Press E-Book and Paperback Original Edition May 2018

Montag Press
ISBN: 978-1-940233-51-2
Design © 2018 Rick Febré

Montag Press Team:
Project Editor – Charlie Franco
Managing Director – Charlie Franco

A Montag Press Book
www.montagpress.com
Montag Press
1066 47th Ave. Unit #9
Oakland CA 94601 USA

Montag Press, the burning book with the hatchet cover, the skewed word mark and the portrayal of the long-suffering fireman mascot are trademarks of Montag Press.

Printed & Digitally Originated in the United States of America
10 9 8 7 6 5 4 3 2 1

"The theory is called that of "many worlds." It is intellectually repulsive, which does not mean it is not true."

John Updike, *Towards the End of Time*

I Ain't Got No Home
in This World Anymore

Mike Sauve

Prologue

I'VE PAID $11.99 for combos in filthy food courts, bodied away against the horror of bygone experience, hoping for something better that isn't going to come. In this way I am like you.

This narrative is a result of too many hours spent in thrall to Facebook memories, primarily the pretty female ones. Though I would carouse with the girls in my real-world waking hours, they came to me in the night while they slept. My name is Sam McQuiggan and for a brief period between the end of 2015 and the beginning of 2016 I was a dream sorcerer. Hello.

The time traveler Sam1 presented an opportunity to address the loneliness and resentment that had somehow spoiled me. I'd reached a point where I would rather evaluate the past than try to build a future. So I would go back. I would murder the phantoms. I would try to fix my selves.

I ENCOUNTERED THE FIRST DOUBLE a few days before Christmas, at about 1:45am, black slush lining the entranceway to Good Feels Fitness and John Cougar Mellencamp singing *I Saw Mommy Kissing Santa Claus* over the sound system.

I felt comfortable at my desk, with my tablet and its anime. Outside I could see people bundled against the cold, regretting their last four beers at Bier Market or another of the Esplanade's big row of yuppie hellholes. I sometimes wondered if the whole craft beer phenomenon wasn't based on posturing rather than palate sophistication. Some things you just want to be a part of. For twenty years I had pretended to enjoy NHL hockey, so I'm not above reproach.

A dozen odd regulars came into the gym during an average graveyard shift, mostly cops and other shift-workers. I knew most by name. I'd toss them a towel or two. We'd talk weather or sports. Sometimes they brought me a coffee. Even one coffee is a day-ruining commitment for me, but I always accepted and then passed it off to Randy the towel guy because coffee is an important social ritual to even the night people who can't tolerate it.

Given the predictable clientele, I was shocked when Sherilyn Drew walked in, even more beautiful than the last time I'd seen her in high school, a time in my life I had not yet recovered from.

My eyes lowered as I touched her card against the sensor and handed her two towels. Encountering a former contemporary would require her to put on a brave face, unable to ask a question innocuous as, "What have you been up to?" because the obvious answer would be, "Pulling in minimum wage at this very Good Feels location, Sherilyn."

Sherilyn didn't show any recognition when I handed back her card. I wasn't surprised. I often ran into people from my hometown of Lac-Sainte-Catherine, and a split-second accord to ignore one another was not uncommon.

She possessed well-proportioned features, pale skin that shone in the good way, and jet black hair pulled into pony tails so tight you wondered if she wasn't doing long-term scalp damage. While well out of my league in high school, at least we'd been in the same broad social orbit. Now she was dressed to the nines and so career-driven she worked out at 1:45 in the morning. And there I was handing out towels. To her it might have seemed our trajectories had ran their natural courses.

When she left for the change room I checked her information on my monitor. Sherilyn Finn. The name looked wrong in the way an old friend or acquaintance's new married name appears strange on Facebook. Though a natural progression into adulthood, it's still a little sad and discomfiting, another thing gone away, meaningless though Sherilyn Drew's last name should have been to me.

I experienced a vocational shame. I wasn't far removed from a respectable job at CLD Finance, copy-writer, 6 am to 2 pm, writing email updates. The death of first one parent and then the other had freed me from that job. Lung cancer took my mom, a non-smoker. A heart attack got my dad a month later. Selling their house and receiving the entirety of a decent insurance policy allowed me to pay off the mortgage on my condo, max out my RRSPs, and start a small fire in my wastebasket at CLD, which had been my way of quitting.

The money wasn't enough to live on forever, so I needed a job. The Good Feels at Yonge and Esplanade had been central to my post-work de-caffeinating process, and also part of my short-lived "work out before work" program. The place was always dead during the overnight shift, and I recognized it as a lazy employee's paradise. A few days later I was working the dream job, reading more than I had in a decade, and sleeping until 5 or 6 pm every day.

Sherilyn left the gym during my fifteen minute break, or so I presumed. At home I opened Facebook and began typing her name. By the time I got to *Sheril* a link popped up for good old *Sherilyn Drew* rather than *Sherilyn Finn*. Her profile said she lived in Vancouver.

A business trip would explain her exercising at a late hour. But the pictures on her Facebook wall could not be explained. There she was, smiling and holding a pint of beer at The Charles Bar in Vancouver. The pictures were tagged only a few hours before she'd made her appearance at Good Feels. Just the flight from Vancouver to Toronto takes at least five hours. I felt an unpleasantness. As if I'd eaten too much popcorn. Then I told myself to get over it, like people leaving a movie theatre tell themselves to get over their terrible post-popcorn lethargy, grossness and self-contempt.

The next day one of the TTC guys brought me a Christmas card. It was a generic one, and he probably gave out hundreds of them, but it brought to mind that I'd receive precious few, what with the parents dead, friends abdicated and alienated, a mouth so salty from my McDonalds' issues, and so on.

More touching was Randy's computer printout inviting

me to a holiday dinner.

> *Dear Sam,*
>
> *My parents and I humbly invite you to Christmas dinner with my family on December 25h Christmas Evening 8pm for traditional Christmas Ham and LCBO. No gift necessary. Please RSVP at convenience.*

Directions to his family home followed. I was sad to recognize his address at 1 Homewood Avenue. One of my classmates had lived there in second year university. The building had only bachelor and one bedroom apartments. The idea of old Randy living in that dump with multiple family members struck a chord, and so I declined his invitation. The only thing sadder than spending Christmas alone would be spending it in the embrace of the Randy family's charity, eating their Ham, drinking their LCBO.

"Out of town," I said.

Randy, whose real name was Ming-húa, but preferred to be addressed by his Canadian name of Randy, wished me a Merry Christmas. I decided to buy him a card or cheap box of chocolates the following day.

A hobo came into the gym, representing one of the job's few challenges. For reasons unknown to me, the downtown homeless shelters had been gifted Good Feels passes to loan out to their constituents on a daily basis. Many were upstanding fellows, just grateful for a shower or a steam room to warm up in. But sometimes the cards got traded around amongst crack addicts desperate to steam the chemicals out of their system for twelve hour periods, which was considered a health hazard, so it was up to me to roust them or call our security contractor if they proved unroustable. This evening's hobo looked pretty jacked up, so I was dreading his inevitable kick out, it being close to Christmas and all.

As I was Googling the contractor's phone number Sherilyn walked in again. This time, with her was our mutual friend Nicole Esposito. Nicole had been close friends with Sherilyn, and something slightly more than friends with me. I'll come right out and admit it. I had been a friend-zoned lackey to her. It's weird, in retrospect, because Nicole didn't possess any of the physical attributes that usually coerce adolescent dudes into the friend zone. She had been cute, and elfish, and I suppose she'd seemed attainable.

She'd grown up down the street from me and we'd played together as children. After the requisite pubescent hiatus we'd been "best friends" for a few years in high school. During this time I had drunkenly professed my love on multiple occasions. She'd demurred politely enough. During a game of spin the bottle once, when her spin landed on me, she'd declined, claiming it would be "weird" because we'd "grown up together," but we'd also grown up with Dave 'Reeder' Reid on Parkview Court and she'd had no qualms when the bottle faced his Batman jaw. On one social occasion near the end of high school she'd told me we could have sex, but it would mean the end of our friendship. I'd accepted the deal; she pretended to have been joking.

We messaged each other about twice a year on Facebook. So unlike Sherilyn she would be forced to acknowledge me. There could be no averting my eyes this time. I steeled myself to provide some cheery explanation regarding my job meant for nineteen year olds. After swiping her card I smiled, but she didn't make eye contact. She continued her conversation with Sherilyn or the fake Sherilyn or whoever it was.

This stung. All the potency of my unrequited need for her, the strength she'd surely drawn from that, the years of putative best friendship, and not even a nod.

I glanced at my screen, expecting to see Nicole Esposito, or Nicole Smith, or Nicole I-Only-Date-Millionaires-Now. That's not what I saw. The name was Leslie Syrup, and that name did not seem real.

·····

The next night Randy handed me an envelope containing a reindeer card and an LCBO gift card for $25 that equalled two hours pay for him. I'd forgotten to get him anything.

"Gee, thanks Randy."

An anorexic semi-regular climbed the Stairmaster for over three hours. I was about to tell her she had to stop (there are regulations about these things) when she tripped and broke her tiny tibia. I called an ambulance and it screamed on up to the Goodfeels entrance and conveyed her to St. Michael's Hospital.

"Merry Christmas," I said to the paramedics.

Randy looked up from his deep web machinations on his laptop and said, "Woman too skinny."

"You got it."

"Too much exercise," he said.

"A palliative to many, a pathology for others."

Randy briefly returned to the surface web to Google *palliative* and then nodded in agreement.

For the third time, the ghosts of my adolescence again entered my Good Feels. This time I looked directly at Nicole.

Stared right into her face more like, defying her to ignore me again. She managed to do so with ease.

"Merry Christmas to you too," I said, eyebrows nearing contact with my hairline as I handed them towels.

They chatted on about some crushed velvet stockings they'd seen on Etsy. As if I'd said nothing. As if I did not exist. They walked into the women's change room and came out in nearly-matching green sports bras. Sherilyn's required no padding other than her own deposits of fatty tissue. Nicole's (Leslie Syrup's?) was padded by foam or maybe some kind of under-wire construction.

On my walk home I mentally composed a dozen angry Facebook messages to Nicole.

"Hey, Syrup, too good to talk to me now? Leslie god-damn Syrup?"

"Care to clarify why you call yourself Leslie Syrup in real life but not on Facebook? Or why you can't even acknowledge my existence?"

"Gym Front Desk guys are people too."

"I don't know why I spent so many years pining for you given your total lack of fatty deposits."

Working nights has a way of distorting one's awareness and prioritization of special days on the calendar. I only remembered it was Christmas Eve when my building's concierge offered a date-specific salutation. This caused me to hold off on my poison pen message to Nicole. It would be inappropriate to spew hatred during a time of year reserved for good tidings. I also wanted to allow for the possibility that it hadn't been her. The chance of two look-a-likes was astronomical, so maybe I was losing it, but then Randy had seen them also, meaning the women were more than figments of my need-rotted psyche.

I watched an old VHS tape of Degeneration X highlights, a Christmas present I'd received at thirteen. Re-invoking that period provided some dull comfort. To this end I also ate a bag of salt and vinegar chips, a snack I'd always enjoyed while watching wrestling movies as a teenager.

As Shawn Michaels and Hunter Hearst Helmsley chopped at their crotches and fellated imaginary dicks I scrolled through Nicole's Facebook photos on my tablet. Halfway through was a picture of her standing next to a personal trainer almost twice her height and width. She looked darling as ever in the same green sports bra I'd seen that night. Except the gym was in Calgary, just like all the content on Nicole's Facebook profile, right up until the previous hour. I put in my mouth guard so that I wouldn't grind my teeth to dust while I slept.

My dreams that night were about the WWE Diva Brie Bella, and skewed prurient, with Brie and I making out in a WWE locker room until the dream took on a labyrinthine complexity of alternate Brie-s in alternate worldlines and alternate me-s in alternate worldlines, and then a whole giant novel's worth of mosaic detail.

There's that moment upon waking from a dream that's like waiting for reality to somehow reset itself. As my reality reset I realized for the first time that something was severely wrong with it.

I started Googling and found myself on the Paranormalis forum reading a post that had five pages of comments dating back to 2010, but then 55 new pages from the previous few days. Here are some selections from the last few pages.

CharlesTreeFort: The number of synchronicities I'm experiencing is off the charts. And other things are way off. My doctor said they're false memories. But she only sees me for like 1.5 minutes at a time because I live in Canada and we have socialized healthcare meaning too many people go to the doctor for little things not like reality breaking down type things which if you ask me are way more important.

Wittgenstein's_Piss_Test: I feel you. Consulting a family doctor in Canada is like trying to talk to a stripper about your feelings after you've paid for the lap dances.

John_Even_Keel: It's like the Many Worlds Theory, but with new cracks between whatever had been keeping the worlds apart. Like why is my sister named Suzanne now? She used to be Rachel. But none of my family will talk to me about it.

HoaxHunterFan: In this thread—endless role playing.

Linda_Moulten_Cow: Remember the time traveler John Titor? A lot of these anomalies sound like the 1% divergence between worldlines he experienced.

Not_Larry_Haber: But in that case the 1% divergence only affected the time traveler. So unless we all travelled through time...

Splendid_Emperor_Xeno: Here's how to dismiss Time Travel in five little words—the earth is always moving. If you travel in time, you'll end up in a place that is not so friendly, like empty fucking space.

OliverWilliamsistheRealJohnTitor: John Titor addresses that pretty comprehensively actually.

Killer_of_Archons134: I believe the archons are behind this.

George_Noory_Sucks: Always the archons with this guy.

TT003: John Titor here. Part of my mandate is to confirm that your reality experience or experientiality has indeed been compromised by irresponsible time travelers. Know that you are not insane.

Dan Scott: Another John Titor that doesn't sound anything like the real John Titor. Great.

HoaxHunterFan: Are you even the same John Titor from like twenty pages ago?

TT_003: No, that one was a fake.

HoaxHunterFan: Oh, that one was a fake. Glad that's cleared up.

It was Sunday afternoon, and I had to be at work in six hours. For the first time I hoped the Sherilyn Drew doppelgangers would come into Good Feels. I was ready to make my move.

On my way to work I saw a man passed out face down on the concrete, an empty bottle of cooking wine by his out-stretched hand. In the past, new to the realities of big city life, I'd have called ambulances for this type of sufferer. But I'd seen it too many times. All a hospitalization would do was delay the booze he'd need upon waking. I shoved the LCBO gift card from Randy in the man's back pocket. He stirred, years in shelters having ingrained in him a need to protect his pockets from thieves. But I was no thief. If the man were conscious he would have thanked me like I was Jolly Old St. Nick for granting him access to whatever his sorrowful version of "the good stuff" was.

My own downward spiral of alcoholic woe widened and commenced its conical menace on the day booze lost me Bethany. In fall semester of my second year at UofT I'd met her at a nightclub called Endocrine. She had been shy and inexperienced, almost deliberately frumpy, wearing baggy blouses that covered an excellent figure. In our months together we'd cuddled on couches, messaged on the then popular MSN Messenger, gone on wild ecstasy and ketamine benders that had advanced our bonding process 2000x. After a failed pull-out attempt we'd walked many city blocks searching for a walk-in clinic open on a civic holiday, needing a morning after pill to nip any and all unwanted offspring in the bud. We'd laughed ironically at reality shows as everyone did then, and for the first time since the comforts of adolescence in L-S-C, I'd felt loved.

I'd been invited to her parents' house that Christmas, and on the verge of entering their lives. By the summer of 2004 we were living together in a tiny attic apartment near Kensington Market. It was the first time either of us had lived with a romantic partner. I remember looking at her one day in our sunny bedroom and thinking, "How privileged I am to have this young wife," just as Oswald must have felt about Marina.

She was kind, and imminently accommodating, and in the right light looked a bit like the young Elizabeth Taylor, but one evening in a fit of rage caused by a dozen hours of drinking I smashed a bunch of plates to make some point and she rightly decided this level of violence was intolerable. She went to a friend's house, called her parents, and I have not seen her since, except on social media websites that are imperative for me not to view. She is not my friend on Facebook, but a number of her profile pictures can be viewed by anyone. The most poisonous one is of her glowing face on the day she married some Quebec-based ski instructor and aspirant Olympic coach.

In the following days and weeks and months I drank

while I studied, drank while I read the standard-issue books for my type. Louis-Ferdinand Céline comes to mind. Blacking out became the norm for me. This term often conveys something worse than it is. I was blacking out in my bed after all. I just wasn't remembering the last hour or two of the night. No big deal. Until one night I didn't black out in my bed, and circumstances landed me in the Don Jail. It was only a drunk and disorderly charge, the property damage charge having been quickly dropped. I was out after a few hours, but the retched thirst upon waking in that cell was what broke me out of my vodka-lubricated descent.

When you drink like I did you get good at off-setting the nightly poisonings. I had a strict routine that involved a yogurt, an egg, two litres of water, and a sauna at the Hart House gym. On that morning, the realization that I could do none of these things was more troubling to me than my incarceration. When a guard passed I asked him for water. He laughed and pointed at the toilet/water fountain. I slumped down on a bench, put my bandaged right hand over my eyes, and wondered if it was possible to die from hangover dehydration.

The legal process was straightforward since I had no record and my dad had promptly paid the store owner $2700 for his window. I was ordered to attend counselling, which I did for a year, hating it the whole time. I quit drinking without detox the moment I left the Don, seizure risk be damned.

The following night at work Randy was afflicted by a nosebleed. He'd bled all over a dozen towels before noticing, and approached me looking heartbroken, holding up two towels like they were the bloody vestments of war.

"Towels destroyed. Punishment?"

Despite repeated assurances to the contrary, Randy was under the false impression that I was his supervisor.

"No punishment necessary pal," I said.

"Both fired!"

Let me briefly interject to say that I am not being condescending towards Randy's dogged pursuit of English-language fluency. I speak about fifty words of broken French, despite studying it for almost twenty years in both high school and university. I'm a firm believer in the dictum that someone speaking poor ESL-English is almost always smarter and more distinguished than anyone so crass as to mock them.

"No one's getting fired. We have like ten thousand towels. No towel audits are conducted."

Randy wouldn't let me just throw the towels in the dumpster out back. He feared the General Manager of our particular location, or worse, the owner of all 349 Good Feels Locations, Happy Gilbin, might inexplicably drop by to inspect the dumpster. There weren't many other options however. Randy suggested we bury the towels beneath a snowbank until he could incinerate them after his shift. But you can't really put anything 'under' a snowbank so much as 'through' the snowbank and in doing so the snowbank grew red with blood and Randy looked like he might start to cry when Sherilyn and Leslie Syrup approached the rear entrance of the building.

"Hello Nicole, or perhaps Leslie. It is I, your long-time friend Samuel McQuiggan."

Nothing.

"Are you really so rude that you can ignore me like this?"

I followed them into the gym and tapped Sherilyn on

the shoulder. No response. I grabbed a towel, twirled it up, and smacked Sherilyn's large but not inelegant butt. They walked right into the change room without even a backwards glance. My craziest occult suspicions were confirmed. They were completely unaware of me. The opportunity to act upon unnoticing parties reminded me of some of my lucid dreams. Most people attempt to fly or meet higher powers upon gaining in-dream consciousness; the few times it's happened to me, to my great discredit, I've always aspired to cozy up to the nearest babe.

The gym was empty. Randy was putting in a fresh load of towels. It took him at least fifteen minutes to fold and bag up the clean ones and get the dirty load started, so there was time. I was given pause when a familiar looking old guy peered in through the Good Feels window wall at me. I couldn't quite place him, nor did I want to, having made some unwholesome acquaintances during the drinking years.

Only the top half of the entrance to the women's change room was visible on camera six. When their workout finished I got down on my hands and knees, and slithered into the change room through this blind spot. It was a calculated risk that no women from the 'real' world with all its concomitant culpabilities would enter the change room while I peeped. Though it would mean my job and criminal charges, that anorexic woman who broke her tibia had been the only regular female patron other than the doubles in the last couple months, plus it had always been a goal of mine to see Sherilyn's naked body. I anticipated a great luminescence.

The girls were in the sauna. I felt like a crazy person opening the cedar door. There had to be some rational reason why they'd ignored me. Now just as the cool air shocked them, so too would my creepy presence,; they'd shriek and I'd face consequences. But there were no screams. They said nothing to me or to one another. I didn't want to dampen my clothing such that I'd have to explain it to Randy, so I retreated, waited a moment on a change room bench, and then ran out in a panic.

I returned to my kiosk and bit my nails for the next twenty minutes. I was relieved when those icons of L-S-C memory-lust left looking fresh and exuberant, hair glistening and pea coats free of detritus as their pea coats somehow always were.

⁙

Three Christmases ago, my mother, something of a new-ager, gave me a Remee Lucid Dream Mask that used light patterns to bother the pons and the parieto-occipital junction and increase the probability of lucid dreaming. It had never worked, and the plastic stitching around the quilting kind of itched at my cheekbones, so it had sat unused in my bathroom cabinet ever since.

On that morning it worked all too well. The dream couldn't accurately be described as *lucid* because I could not manipulate the in-dream reality; still it was exceptional, a perfectly vivid, 100% realistic experience. It felt not like a manifestation of my subconscious but rather a different me in a different place, you know, just walking around and talking to people. It's here that I'm afraid we've reached a level of abstraction about the nature of waking vs. dreaming consciousness that I'm not qualified to discuss in much depth.

Another deviation from my normal dream protocol was my ability to type all of it up minutes after waking in a state of terror, and 359 experiential years later, as I'm writing this narrative, all I had to do was a quick search of my hard drive to find it:

It starts in my empty childhood home with my parents looking bereft. This seems informed by the last episode of Growing Pains *and also the last episode of* The Fresh Prince of Bel-Air, *where the main characters stand in an empty house, or on an empty set, and the house or set is revealed to be nothing more than a prop brought to life by the players that toed its boards. My mom asks if I'm okay. "Not hungover enough," I respond, and all the family laughs. Pay attention to any functioning alcoholic's repertoire of hangover humour, and you'll find little more than, "Hangover's are a dickens aren't they—something we all go through, not the near entirety of my existence or anything."*

Then it transitions to some kind of party or pub night scenario with all my lost high school friends. I greet Donny and Little Ray and Scooze who would go on to Paralympic success, and lo there's even Dave 'Reeder' Reid and it's just like old times. There's a strong sense of all this wasted time, and all this unrealized potential for camaraderie, like, 'Why did I wait so long to reconnect with these guys?'

Bethany is still or again my girlfriend, and in attendance. All the perfect girls of your life are one in dreams, all the 'great long-remembered dances' become one dance. We're drinking Coronas and the old gang is laughing at a story I'm telling about putting. There's this grand sense of all the history we'd shared, and at its core is a confirmation of whatever long-expired goodness of mine that had drawn laughs in suburban basements and later drawn Bethany to me.

I look at Bethany and experience an aching feeling because a part of me recognizes that this is a dream and that Bethany is gone.

I bump into some meathead who doesn't have many kind words. There's a real unhealthy compulsion towards exercise in L-S-C, where young men make temples out of the body to compensate for the atrophy of the mind.

"There he is," says Mark Drew.

Bethany looks around nervous. A 'What-has-he-done-now?'-kind of look.

"There's the guy who's been spying on my sister."

Mark and a beefier sort grab me and start shaking me around.

"You think it's okay to break into the women's change room at The Dewey B. Larsen Centre?"

I am carted off to jail. This scene is similar to the real-life one in which I woke without water, but now there's the realization of a fifteen-year prison sentence, and this overwhelming weight on me like, "How am I going to get through fifteen years in this lightless place eating grade-d pork and maybe should I just start looking at suicide options now."

The dream concludes with Bethany visiting me. She's crying, her hand pressed against the Plexiglas window that separates us.

"I'm sorry I let you down," I say.

"It's okay."

"Tell me this isn't real."

"It's real."

"Tell me I can just wake up from this."

I woke up from it. I meditated on my sorrow. I threw the lucid dream mask in the garbage can by my nightstand, feeling a twinge of panic.

While consequence-free at my own particular Good Feels, the dream had me worried that alternate Sams, perhaps working at alternate versions of L-S-C's Dewey B. Larsen Centres, that were paying the price in alternate L-S-Cs.

I texted Randy for help. I asked him if he knew how to hack a Facebook account.

"Is this...*ultimatum*?"

"I wouldn't say *ultimatum*, no," I wrote. "More like a favour."

"You give me all information. I will go behind seven

proxies. Safe to do this way."

After scanning the girls' profiles to refresh my memory I gave him what I could: Dates of birth, names of pets and parents, hometown, etc. Randy's script cracked Nicole's account in less than one second. He revealed her password had been the hilariously weak *Nicole123*.

"Don't do anything she'll notice. Arrested by police and deported from Canada is my fear," he wrote.

The third message in Nicole's inbox was between her and Sherilyn. I scrolled back to December 27th, a few days after I'd encountered the first doubles.

Sherilyn: Babeeeeeeeeeeeeeeeeeeeeeeeeeeeeee!

Nicole: Hi gorgeous. We haven't talked in so long. I thought you'd abandoned me. ;(

Sherilyn: Never!

Nicole: We need to have a Skype date soon!

Sherilyn: I know!

Nicole: Did you see that Jeneatte Seberg is marrying JP Belmont?

Sherilyn: I'm afraid so. Shouldn't there be like a six hundred pound combined weight limit for potential marriage partners?

Nicole: I can't wait to see the pictures.

Sherilyn: Even Kirk Mattingly won't be able to make them look unhideous.

Nicole: Pop quiz hotshot, you are getting married in L-S-C, but Kirk Mattingly isn't available to take your wedding photos because he is shooting fifteen other L-S-C weddings that day. What do you do?!?

Sherilyn: Kill my potential partner and learn to love again, for why wed if it can't be documented by L-S-C's star wedding photographer?

Nicole: You think someone else would step up to fill that void.

Sherilyn: Too busy financing their Oxy addictions I'm guessing.

Nicole: I think it's Fentanyl now, but yeah, how did L-S-C go downhill so fast?

Sherilyn: Oxy, or Fentanyl, I guess.

Nicole: Remember how rare it was to see a homeless person when we were kids? Like my dad would see one and there'd be this race to see which do-gooder could get him a banana and a ham sandwich first.

Sherilyn: Yeah, last time I was home there were at least six junkies just hanging around the library. Then an ambulance had to come and pick one of them up.

Nicole: Lol.

Sherilyn: I feel bad for Daniela though and the rest of them who never made it out.

Nicole: Yeah, like Daniela is still so pretty but who can she find to marry there that will meet her epic standards?

Sherilyn: So….Remember Sam McQuiggan?

Nicole: How could I forget? He still messages me like 100 times a year.

Sherilyn: Eww.

Nicole: I know.

Sherilyn: I would unfriend someone like that. Why is he still thinking about you if he hasn't talked to you or seen you in ten years?

Nicole: I know but his parents just died so I feel bad.

Sherilyn: ☹ He probably has some creepy shrine to you though.

Nicole: Eww don't say that. Anyway, what about him?

Sherilyn: I swear to God, like five nights in a row I've had these super weird dreams about him.

Nicole: Ewwww.

Sherilyn: Yeah, and it's always the same. Like he's at the Dewey B. Larsen Centre and we're getting it on in the change room. Or, more like he's getting it on while I'm just standing there. You were in one of them too. But he wasn't messing with you. And your name was like Leslie Pancake or something.

Nicole: Hahahhahaah! Oh my God you are going to divorce Rick and Kirk Mattingly will be shooting memory card after memory card of you and Sam.

Sherilyn: In Sam's dreams.

Nicole: In your dreams it sounds like! Actually, you know what though, I did suddenly remember all this weird stuff about him right when I was falling asleep the other night.

Sherilyn: Sam McQuiggan, Invader of Dreams.

Nicole: Good old Sammy, with his acne and halitosis, your locker room lover 4 life.

Sherilyn: Gross.

And with that, I decided it was about time for a goddamn drink.

The Liquor Control Board of Ontario outlets didn't open until 11 am. Believe it or not, that is what folks in Ontario call their liquor marts. To kill time I browsed through the Occult section at Chapters for an hour, bought some limes and club soda at Loblaws, and then ate a McDonald's breakfast with no concern for its pestilential salt content. Nothing relieves a dry or salty mouth like a couple dozen vodka-sodas, like mouthwash for the soul.

I bought a sixty ounce bottle, which had always been the best value, but also represented a depressing commitment to prolonged drinking. The price increase irked me. Several years previous they'd been as low as $45. Now they were $59.85. In the U.S. you could get one for $20. Here is the tyranny of socialized Liquor Control.

In my kitchen I poured two shots into a tumbler, splashed some soda in and squeezed a lime wedge over it. I prepared to experience physical and spiritual refreshment. Instead I nearly gagged. It was and always would be just ethanol. An actual poison to the human body. I mixed in more soda, and by the third drink it was like old times.

Also like old times was my immediate awareness of the clock and how long I could continue drinking for and still get a reasonable amount of sleep. I had to be up by 11 pm to shower and walk to work. That meant falling asleep by 5 pm for a mere six hours. I'd learned a dangerous fact during my drinking days: drunkards with elevated body temperatures get their REM sleep immediately if at all, meaning all restorative sleep occurs in the first four hours, with any subsequent hours usually spent tossing and turning in a desperate attempt to fall back asleep. Employing this terrible logic, I ended up drinking until 7 pm, and barely made it to my bed before landing face down. Being out of practise, I hadn't even put a glass of water on the nightstand.

My alarm rang. With vision still blurry, I mixed a double, drank it, and then nursed a second one in the shower. I also filled a water bottle with equal parts vodka and soda and stuck it in my school bag, prepared to drink it warm throughout the day as necessity might dictate.

Outside my condo sat that same menacing old guy who'd

been looking into Good Feels, with his hood pulled up and a scarf covering half of his face. He stared right at me. Though reasonably willing to assist the dispossessed, and there being nothing overtly frightening or depressing about this guy, I felt a strong compulsion to look away.

"What?" I asked him.

"What?" he said back, the time-honoured dance of aggressive jerks.

I picked up the pace.

At work, Randy asked, "Sick?"

"Just tired."

"You look sick."

"Just tired," I said, "Didn't sleep well."

There was nothing to do but feel sorry for myself and rub at my left side. I drank as much water as I could and eventually asked Randy to watch the front desk while I used the bathroom. Instead I went for a fifteen minute steam. Given the additional fifteen minutes it took to undress, shower, and towel off, Randy looked worried when I returned.

"About to rescue if needed, but could not leave post."

"You did good Randy. A bit of bowel trouble is all."

"See doctor. Free healthcare in Canada. Good living standard."

"I'll give it a couple days. I appreciate the concern though."

Though fate may be complicit in the bad decisions of all men, it is demonstrably and undeniably complicit in the bad decisions of all drunks. Sherilyn and Nicole came in at 7:10 am, hours later than their previous visits, and just before my shift was to end.

Severe hangovers had always produced a dramatic uptick in the depravity of my desires. Screw the dream world, I thought, I am going to get mine. At worst a proposition would have no impact on them, at best, they would be as open to suggestion as any actor in a lucid dream. After they'd showered and were on their way out I touched Sherilyn's elbow.

"My shift is almost over. Please sit down and wait for me to finish," I said, leading her to a chair. She sat showing no emotion, like she was waiting at the dentist's office in a dream.

"You can go," I said to Nicole. She went.

Randy did not look happy to see me leaving with the mystery girl who'd been haunting our shifts. My front desk replacement Candy was chipper as ever though. Good Feels has no policies about romantic involvement with clientele, as that would deter the teen employee base.

I led Sherilyn down Yonge Street and past the concierge at my condo. I'd worried she might say something to expose me, but she was silent, and wore a default look of contentment. The strong drink I'd packed hadn't been touched, so the first thing I did was pour it over a huge pile of ice.

"Drink?" I asked the Sherilyn-thing.

I put on a Muddy Waters record and ran through my in-brain database of Sherilyn-specific memories. I could recall a time she'd asked me for a piggyback ride. This recollection caused my more lecherous instincts to fade, and I thought, 'Hey, it might be nice just to have this charming presence in the old condo all the time.' While she didn't have much to say, she smelled fantastic and had that skin we'd all wanted to touch so much. I pressed the back of my hand against her cheek. What a fine cheek. I started caressing her thigh, and the thickness there moved my thoughts to a more simian place. I tried removing her fuzzy green sweater, but pulling it off her was like pulling a sweater off a mannequin, except worse because I had to flail her arms around and at one point inadvertently hit her in the mouth with her own elbow.

What length of prison term might the dream-world Sam face for this? Was it selfish of me to rob from him in this way? It was like that Seinfeld joke about staying up too late: It's not his problem. The tiredness will be Morning Jerry's problem. That joke holds particular resonance for all working drunks. I paused to consider. Given the recent malleable nature of worldlines or whatever I didn't want to do anything ethically dubious.

After another giant drink I made a plan. My building had a beautiful pool I rarely used, being too embarrassed to be seen there alone. Others went alone, but they were swimming laps, not just splashing around or sitting solitary in the hot tub looking morose and without purpose. I led her to the elevator, onto the street, and a block east to a Sportchek where I bought her a medium one-piece bathing suit. She'd had the sports bra/shorts combo in her gym bag, but wearing something like that to a pool just wasn't the Sherilyn Drew way.

Uncertain if I could expect her safe return from the pool's change room, I put the bathing suit on her in my living room. The functional necessity of this made me feel slightly less worried for alternate Sams, even if I did take my time and one piece bathing suits traditionally require some finagling to stretch onto a curvy body. Sherilyn's breasts, not aided by the expensive bras she owned, weren't as perfect as anticipated. One was a little smaller, with some indescribable areola anomaly that did not affect the larger breast; still, one must accept the eccentricity of areolae, so overall—not half bad.

In the hot tub I drank vodka-soda from a coffee cup, even though in-hot tub imbibing is discouraged and frequently threatened against by property management. I held her hand. The sun shone in through the glass doors to the patio, and I laughed, because this was the happiest I'd felt in years.

"This is fun," I said to her.

She smiled, empty.

"We'll have to do this again sometime," I said.

I positioned her in the shower in my condo, peeled the bathing suit from her, and dried her off. I resisted the urge to take a picture. I was tired, and felt satiated for the first time in years. I put her clothes back on and led her to the street, having decided that keeping her in the condo would raise a whole number of problematic temptations.

"Bye," I said. "You should come to Good Feels around the same time tomorrow."

I gave her a little nudge northward back to whatever ghostly place she inhabited when not a part of my personal experience.

After sleeping better than I had in months, I woke up and checked Nicole's Facebook messages.

Sherilyn: Okay this is getting weird….

Nicole: What?

Sherilyn: I had another dream about Sam.

Nicole: Just stop thinking about him. You had a dream, so you thought about him, now you're having more dreams. Think about Alatragus Pino or someone hotter lol!

Sherilyn: This was like the realest dream I ever had. I'm not even sure if it was a dream…

Nicole: You're being crazy……… ;)

Sherilyn: No, this was like my real life. Like I am living some kind of other life with Sam, in my dreams…haha

Nicole: Well I'm not a psychologist but tell me what happens in the dreams.

Sherilyn: Sam is living with me in my parents' house in L-S-C. And this goes on, and on, and on. Have you ever had a dream that felt like it lasted for years?

Nicole: I don't think so.

Sherilyn: Like Sam is going with me to the Central Mall to buy batteries, Sam is shovelling the driveway, Sam is playing UNO with me and my parents.

Nicole: It could be worse. It could be Steve Spinula.

Sherilyn: Oh my god this isn't funny!

Nicole: Sorry I just don't see what the big deal is. Everyone has weird dreams sometimes.

Sherilyn: I'm looking at his Facebook photos now…. and here's the weirdest part….in the dream I distinctly remember him wearing like this red windbreaker. There are barely any pictures of him on Facebook, but in the only one from the last few years he's wearing a red windbreaker.

Nicole: I think he works at a gym or something.

Sherilyn: Tell me he doesn't work at Good Feels.

Nicole: I think he does.

Sherilyn: This is messed up. I swear I had no way of knowing that except for this dream. It was this combination of Good Feels and the Dewey B. Larsen Centre in L-S-C.

Nicole: Okay weirdooooooo.

Sherilyn: Fuck you.

Nicole: Are you kidding me right now>

Sherilyn: Sorry.

Nicole: Don't swear. It scares me when my baby swears

Sherilyn: Maybe I will send him a message on Facebook.

Nicole: Don't do that. The more you think about him, the more dreams probably.

Sherilyn: Maybe it will burst the bubble—like "see, nothing to Sam…just a guy working pathetically at a gym who's a little less ugly than he was in high school."

Nicole: LOL.

Sherilyn: Think I should?

Nicole: Why not? Maybe at least then he'll leave me alone.

It would have been interesting to send Sherilyn a message saying something like, "Getting batteries at the central mall babe, what kind do we need," but I was on thin ice as it was vis-à-vis interdimensional dream sorcery ethics.

          ⁘

I bought an orange. I arrived at work forty-five minutes early so I could go for a steam. Steam induced hyperthermia, strengthening my immune system and drawing toxins out through my skin. I began to feel something like good cheer. Hangovers, or more accurately, the eventual recovery from them, had always produced in me a curious feeling of psychological well-being.

When Randy saw me he said, "Looking much better today. Healed by doctor."

"Yeah," I said, "Yeah."

The girls arrived at 7 am again. I greeted them with enthusiasm, watched them work out, and when they were finished I left Good Feels with a memory on each arm. I couldn't decide who smelled better. I might have given a slight edge to Nicole had my opinion of her not been jaundiced by excessive time spent in the friend zone.

In my condo I guided them to the couch and made myself a drink. I'd never had an issue with drinking alone; in most cases I even preferred it, but I made them both a sugary cocktail to be a good host.

"Drink up," I said.

"Why?" asked Sherilyn.

"Or don't. It's really your call."

"Why are we here?" asked Nicole.

"To have a good time," I said, "Just a short visit."

Things got hazy from that point on.

I woke to a pounding on the door. My sound system blared the Woody Guthrie song *I Ain't Got No Home in this World Anymore* at max volume. Though thematically about economic hardship rather than romantic loss, this was the maudlin tribute to Bethany I played on repeat during my ugliest binges. After racing to the pause button I noticed Sherilyn lying facedown on the couch. I rolled her over to see if she was alive. She was, although her mascara had run down her face and she looked awful. I threw a blanket over her. I opened the door a crack.

"Sorry to bother you," said a neighbour I couldn't recall having seen before, "Your music has been super loud for like five hours. I don't normally complain because I like loud music too sometimes and it is the middle of the day, but I was actually getting kind of worried because it sounded like the same song the whole time."

I generated as much generosity as it was prudent to fake. "You know what? I work nights, so when I fall asleep nothing can wake me. I must have fallen asleep with that song playing. So so sorry," I said, and smiled like a big stupid Canadian.

"Oh no problem. Sorry for bothering you. Hope I didn't wake you up."

"Don't be sorry, that must have been annoying."

"Okay, well glad everything is fine. Sorry again."

"It's okay!"

The level of the bottle revealed that I'd consumed at

least twenty ounces, assuming Sherilyn or old Syrup hadn't put any back after the introductory drinks. Nicole's state was worse than Sherilyn's. A lampshade had been placed over her head. When I removed the lampshade I laughed through my nose. Not a mirthful laugh, but the muted laugh laughed by drunks the world over when waking to the damages they've inflicted. Beneath the lampshade was a creamy white substance. I had pie-faced her in the face with a frozen lemon meringue pie from my freezer.

Twenty ounces, I thought. In the bad old days this would have been standard operating procedure, but I was out of practise. I groaned, experiencing a full body revulsion only slightly offset by being half drunk. Casual drinkers can look forward to the alleviation of their symptoms as the day progresses. Those who are frequently still drunk in the morning know they must sink to the depths of sorrow valley before trudging slowly up into a condition of moderate well-being. But as previously mentioned, that period of ascension, freedom from the soul symptoms of a real hangover, is actually quite a fine feeling.

I propped Sherilyn up and said, "I'm sorry. I'm so sorry," and meant it. I wiped her mascara with a wet paper towel but only managed to spread it around and make it worse. I wiped the lemon meringue off poor Leslie Syrup. I tried to think of a joke involving pancake makeup and lemon meringue, since they were both white, but failed. Downstairs I bid them goodbye.

"Maybe you better stay away from Good Feels for a while," I said, and nudged them on their way.

The worst revelation greeted me when I re-entered my condo. I woke my laptop from its sleep and saw a profile picture of Bethany glowing out 678 kilobytes worth of beauty.

No wonder I'd been playing *I Ain't Got No Home In This World Anymore* on repeat. Beneath Bethany was something far worse. Five pictures of Dave Reid arranged atop a pentagramic template I must have imported into Photoshop.

I logged into Nicole's Facebook account because why not, you know?

Nicole: Okay, I don't want to freak you out…

Sherilyn: Sam?

Nicole: Sam and fucking whip cream pies or something?

Sherilyn: Elaborate.

Nicole: I have this dream where Sam is wheeling me in a big vat of pies and you're sitting there crying.

Sherilyn: This is messed up.

Nicole: Did you have that dream?

Sherilyn: No actually, I enjoyed a rare respite from Sam last night. This time it was Dave Reid strung up on a crucifix or something.

Dave Reid had lived and ate the same overcooked roasts with me, shared my Nintendo and then Super Nintendo, and slept in my bedroom on about eighty percent of nights between the years of 1989 and 1995, years in which we grew from six to twelve. The arrangement began when his mom's cancer had reached the terminal stage, and his dad was spending most nights at the hospital with her. In one of those cruel larcenies from recollection, I can't for the life of me recall what kind of cancer she had.

As infant neighbours, we'd been de facto best friends for years before that, but over all those pork and bean afternoons, all those post-bedtime whisperings, we'd become something closer to brothers. We attended the same elementary school and during that first year when his mom was sick we were seated next to each other by a random seating plan. We played with the other kids, but we'd also walk furious laps around the school together, plotting schemes to steal my dad's four-wheeler and take it out on some midnight spree, or smuggle the Sears catalogue into my room so we could look at Sears-tier braziers by flashlight.

Dave's mother died in 1992. I recall standing a row behind him at the funeral. We wore identical blue suits that my mom had purchased two-for-one at Moore's. Dave wasn't crying at first, which I admired, but then Dave's father Alexander started to not so much cry as shriek. When Dave then lost it, it was my mother's arms he fell into. That got me going and soon even my dad was sobbing and scrunching up his eyes to hold back the pain.

His father got piss drunk at the post-funeral reception and so Dave slept at our house that night. No one held this against Dave's dad, who'd been upstanding in his long vigil for his wife. It was expected that soon Dave's things would be packed up and he'd no longer be spending nights with us. But Dave's dad didn't stop drinking after the post-funeral reception. Dave's dad was more or less drunk from that point on. He wasn't a cruel drunk, and I never heard him yell or anything. I'd see him stumbling around his immaculate backyard, listening to The Grateful Dead, jovial in the afternoons, unable to stand by evening. My parents weren't the type to call children's aid or meddle in a neighbour's affairs. L-S-C suburbanites seldom locked their doors, so my mother would go over after her shift at the dental office, bring Alexander some leftovers, and if he wasn't already at our place, she'd invite Dave over for dinner. Never so much an invitation as a corralling.

Together we'd watch *Perfect Strangers* and lie in my bed; when puberty encroached we spoke of those girls first to establish tits while stroking our yet useless boners. Every morning my dad told an elaborate bullshit story at breakfast that we took to calling "the state of breakfast address." By the sixth grade Dave began to excel at sports, and had grown handsome. He was always the first pick in baseball or basketball at recess, where I was always picked toward the end. Through this disparity he stuck by me, elevating me to his social status by mere proximity. I appreciated this, but it also generated in me an ugly dependence on him. If he spent time after school with a group of other boys I became jealous. He absorbed this with more maturity than could be expected of any twelve year old, never lashing out or plotting to abandon me.

In the eighth grade Alexander fell into my father's shed and asked for help. A day later he was in L-S-C's lone detox. Two weeks later he was in rehab. Three months later he was back in his home and healed. Dave no longer had to sleepover so frequently. He still did a couple nights a week, but it was only social, just like he also slept over at the homes of his other friends. Sometimes I was invited to these external sleepovers, and sometimes I wasn't, and on the times I wasn't it killed me.

Sensing the fragility of my bond with Dave and its inevitable severing, my mother sought to give me a sense of identity by enrolling me in a theatre camp near Sault Ste. Marie. I didn't emerge from that theatre camp a homosexual, but by L-S-C's standards of masculinity I might as well have. I emoted, enunciated, and may have worn a scarf at some point. A picture from a production of *Rosencrantz and Guildenstern are Dead* shows me in way too much eyeliner (which is required in theatre because of the lights, but is always way overdone by amateurs) with an honest-to-God snake around my neck. I would have fit right in at Andy Warhol's Factory as one of his youthful concubines.

All while Dave continued to excel at sports, the surest route to popularity and sexual prosperity in L-S-C, which also was our world. He played on the high school football and soccer teams, and the student body graced him with the unoriginal but potent nickname of Reeder (usually spoken with a prolonged *eeee* and 'greasy' rolled *rs*.) Though still neighbours, it grew difficult for me to encroach on his time. When I dropped by his place a throng of defensive linemen would be there eating pizza. Maybe Dave would give me one of his slices while everyone else ate five and the discussion rarely veered from nickel packages, meaning I couldn't exactly be like "Hey, remember those childhood nights that formed us, Reeder?"

In grade eleven Alexander remarried and the family moved to the west end of town. In one of those millions and millions of unheralded tragedies that affect the young, our friendship was reduced to the occasional nod in the hallway, the occasional sentence or two of recognition in the cafeteria line, as though we had never shared the things we'd shared, the nights and mornings in front of the mirror with our toothbrushes. No one, not even Bethany, has occupied so cruel and persistent a place in my dreams. Almost every night I dream of reunion with Dave, not Reeder, but Dave. There's a sad question on my mind almost every morning. And it's so pathetic and gross that I almost choke on it. It's "Why have we been away from each other for so long? Dave? My brother?"

---- **10** ----

That night Randy and I played Scrabble on our phones. He usually won because he spent hours reading the dictionary each night and could score impressive bingos.

After winning on a lucky triple word score, I put my head down and decided to stop thinking about Nicole and Sherilyn. This would banish them. Then in came some version of Bethany on the bulky arm of Dave 'Reeder' Reid.

I swallowed a bunch of times. I tried to avert my eyes. I considered abandoning my post altogether. But Randy was wheeling his big towel cart away from the welcome station at the very worst time.

This Bethany had aged well, with only the earliest indication of a double chin in the works. This Dave had packed on at least eighty extra pounds of muscle. He looked menacing, like he might throw a tackle at any minute. His eyes contained none of the light they'd had in childhood, but then neither did mine.

To be ignored by Bethany after all those nights of drunken tribute to her image would be painful. Some automaton Bethany might be worse. Still worse yet was what happened. Her face registered some approximation of wonder.

"Sam!" she said.

"Hello Bethany."

My voice sounded too sweet. I looked to Dave. It wasn't fear of flirting with this monstrous man's love interest that bothered me; it was sounding feminine in front of my very arch model of maleness.

"Oh my God, Sam!" said Bethany, needing to say something.

She looked like she might cry. Dave Reid rocked back on his feet in the fashion of athletes everywhere, not revealing too many cards, maybe not even possessing cards, maybe all the testosterone released by his regimen having granted him freedom from sentiment-inducing hormones.

She gave me a clumsy hug across the kiosk. I pressed my palm against her neck for a second too long. Here was my missing girl, my young wife and friend. All present in that ugly moment under the fluorescent lights of Good Feels.

"How have you been?" she asked.

"Not bad."

"Wow, I can't believe it," she said, enunciating each word.

She was trying.

"Hey Dave," I said.

"Hey man," said Dave.

Dave and I had severed communications after an unfortunate series of drunken Facebook messages I'd sent him. More accurately he had deleted me from his Facebook.

"Sorry about the weird Facebook messages Dave," I said, "And for everything else."

"Relax man, it's cool," said Dave.

As Thomas McGuane once wrote, "Telling someone to relax is not as aggressive as shooting them, but it's up there."

Dave looked at his watch.

"We better go get changed," Bethany said. "It was so nice seeing you."

How many tragic run-ins like this in the average year, globally? An expired love spotted at a crosswalk and greeted with a nod, quick hello, or an "Oh my God!" that expresses surprise but not much else. I felt anger at the brief happiness I'd had. Without the relationship's hours of blissful congress there wouldn't be any feeling, which must sound trite, but really, I bet all those smiling rubes on the streetcar lead milquetoast lives from birth to death and never feel much of anything one way or the other, and that's why they can affect contentment so easy. It may even be possible that they are genuinely content.

I looked at their names on my screen, not wanting them to be real. Her name was Bethany Reid. His name was Dave Reid. I would have preferred Bethany Bagel and Dave Breakfast-Sandwich. At least they'd come from different sectors of my personal history, requiring a massive coincidence for the two unrequited loves of my life, fraternal and romantic, to end up together and up in my Good Feels business. I chose to believe they weren't real. A few days of not thinking about them and they'd leave me alone.

I kept an eye on Dave and Bethany's workout. Dave squatted hundreds of pounds while Bethany mirrored him with less weight. My eyes stung with sadness and rage after he slapped her on the butt to conclude their final set. On their way out, Dave said, "Seeya man," as though we'd last seen each other only a few days ago. Bethany gave me a little wave and an apologetic look.

At home I drank straight from the bottle, something I rarely did even in my darkest days. I heated some chicken fingers in the T-Fal Actifry I'd inherited from my parents, but all the breading ended up crumbling away from the ugly grey chicken foundation. It was the little things. Bethany had prepared food with tremendous skill during our short time together. Whereas my modest food preparations often ended in this type of failure. I punched the T-Fal Actifry until I cut my hand on one of its space age components.

Recognizing an uptick in drunken sloppiness, I mixed a revivifying vodka and Redbull and opened my laptop. Pentagramically-crucified Dave Reid greeted me. I minimized Photoshop and deleted the file, hoping this would delete Dave from my life in the process.

I needed to reach out to someone. Scanning my mental rolodex, there wasn't one person who'd respond to an early morning "How are you doing?" from me, let alone a message detailing my bizarre tale of doppelgangers run amok. I decided to share my story on the Paranormalis reality glitch thread. My post told of Sherilyn's anomalous appearance, of old flames lacking in agency, and of my cosmic transgressions. That sapped all my energy. Or more likely the booze did, so I went to sleep. After a couple hours I woke shaking and unable to get back to sleep. I checked the responses to my thread on Paranormalis.

Anonymous User: Very interesting post. I wonder if the close friend and love interest are more autonomous because they occupied a more significant place in the OP's life.

Skellington: Did you hit that girl in the face with a pie as a symbolic face-cumming. And since given the opportunity why not a legit face-cumming?

John_Hogue's_Hoagie: This is the craziest account yet, with the possible exception of that guy whose Corolla turned into a snow blower even though he lived in Florida and he was like, 'What am I supposed to do with this?'

Wittgenstein's_Piss_Test: That guy started a Kickstarter for a new car about an hour later. I'm pretty sure he was scamming us.

Not_Larry_Haber: One of the Titors must have big

plans for the OP.

The Ghost of D. Skrellman: Not the Titor stuff again. OP, just a heads up, there's like four or five RPers on this board who keep saying John Titor has contacted them. It's best to hide all their comments so this otherwise significant thread doesn't devolve into role play.

Not_Larry_Haber: Look, some of us have been contacted by John Titor(s) and think that's what this is all about.

The Ghost of D. Skrellman: And some of us aren't role-playing.

Not_Larry_Haber: Whatever skep-dick. OP, has John Titor contacted you?

The Ghost of D. Skrellman: [Link to 18 Page *John Titor Fucked Up Reality You Guise* thread.]

..... ·1 ·1 .....

I checked my email and at the top was a message from John_Titor001001@gmail.com

I'd been introduced to the fictionalized version of John Titor by the anime series *Steins;Gate*, leading me to the cultish websites that chronicled the 'real' Titor's incredible story, his faxes to Art Bell, his pull-out drawing (see below) of a time machine that would have taken hours for even a pro to draw. If Titor's predictions weren't made by a time traveler, then they were written by a team of physics wonks and probably a talented sci-fi author or two (Robert Silverberg and David Brin have been suggested). He predicted VOIP, cultural trends like YouTube, and that Project Ginger would yield the Segway when all of that information was hard to come by.

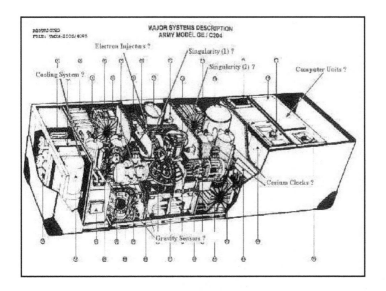

I had to blink hard several times as I read the email.

Dear Mr. Samuel McQuiggan

Allow me to sincerely apologize for the imperson-al nature of this correspondence. Best practises in these situations call for long term counselling. Regrettably, TimeMind Industries have damaged the structural integrity of your worldline so substantially that there isn't sufficient time to address individual issues with our usual rigour.

Here's the hard truth. Several time travelers from an alternate worldline's 2037 have reached your time-line. These were among the earliest private contractors. One of them was an alternate version of you, Samuel

McQuiggan. Also born in 1983, also with a history of alcoholism, also 5'11, etc. etc.

With the proper oversight Sam1's arrival would cause no complications for you, whom we refer to as the dual occupant. Somewhat confusingly, the time traveler Sam McQuiggan is also known as a dual-occupant. To avoid misidentification, he we will be referred to as Sam1, while you will be referred to as Sam2. This may be offensive to you, as one's own personal experience will always take primacy. Try to see it from my perspective. I come from 2045, eight years after Sam1 left for your worldline. I was not aware of you until I became aware of him. I have just recently been made aware of you. One facet of the Many Worlds Interpretation even argues this worldline didn't exist until Sam2 or the first of his cohorts arrived here. But that's not something we should get into.

The reason for my high work volume is that Time-Mind's Sony Gravity Distortion Unit was rushed into service and full of bugs. An easily preventable glitch sent many of TimeMind's original trial subjects back to this specific (#29435654534690900949228484341126115111011432...) worldline, one after the other, creating a problematic glut. This is a historic case of malfeasance wherein not only does the time traveler experience a divergence from his known reality, the dual-occupant (you; Sam2) does as well.

Far worse, far far worse, is in this case a ripple effect has led to universal confusion and dissonance for even this worldline's single occupants, e.g. the thing with the Corolla, etc.

By the time of my first mission these types of bugs

had been long since rectified, and these early mistakes were swept under the rug in the name of progress. A more compassionate leadership came into power in 2044 however, and they have pledged reconciliation. I am here to allay your concerns. This allaying of concerns is considered the most basic human right. If necessary, I will also help you seek compensation for any wrongdoing Sam1 may inflict. One of the most serious accusations against TimeMind involves the improper vetting of their initial subjects. The term "clueless guinea pig" has been thrown around. Compounding the issues you'll face is that your dual-occupant has turned out to be an unreliable asshole. Early reconnaissance reveals Sam1 has been blind drunk during the majority of his waking hours on your worldline.

Rest assured that I plan to detain him at my earliest opportunity. Unfortunately, I am dealing with about a dozen individuals, some of whom could well rupture the very fabric of this worldline at any moment, and since Sam1 seems to be just drunk or sleeping it off most of the time he is low on my list of priorities.

You may well wonder why I'd write such a long email if I'm so busy. My answer is that I'm taking a lot of what you might style "future amphetamines with no real downside" to get this job done and as a result rarely get an email written in under 1500 words these days.

Please contact me if you need any advice, or to take the first steps in a grievance process against Samuel McQuiggan1, an established contractor of Time-Mind Inc.

For your benefit I have attached links explaining the Everett-Wheeler model, some essential time travel specs involving Kerr Holes and Tipler effects, the complete John Titor posts, and forms on which you can detail adverse effects resultant of the negligent actions of TimeMind if you so choose. In my experience, your best bet is to try and maintain a sense of humour about all of this.

Best Regards,
Major John Titor

Office of Temporal Human Resources

Still quite drunk, I responded with total credulity.

Wow, I can't believe they send the real John Titor back to interface with me. Huge fan of your work!.

He wrote back a few minutes later.

I must confess I'm not actually the real John Titor. We find that the John Titor brand has taken hold in much of the superverse and lends credence to our correspondence. My real name is Chuck. Godspeed Sam2.

And while I have your attention…what are the best over-the-counter downers for a man in my position? I'm Googling it and the answer seems to be NyQuil cold syrup? Can this be right?

I wrote back.

Yeah, try NyQuil. I'd suggest getting blackout drunk but the Liquor Control Board of Ontario just closed until 11 am tomorrow morning.

.....:1 :2:.....

What could a dual-occupant do? I tossed and turned for two hours before leaving for work. Standing on the other side of Yonge Street was the man who'd glared in at me through the Good Feels window and accosted me near the entrance to my condo. He crossed the intersection and gripped my shoulder.

"Jesus Christ, you look about as bad as I feel," I said.

"Hello Irishman," said Sam McQuiggan1.

As the McQuiggan moniker must illustrate, I'm of Irish heritage, though it wasn't a big part of my experience growing up. We didn't sit around the McQuiggan home reading Joyce or eating potatoes or sipping Jameson or whatever the nuclear Irish family is presumed to do. If an unfamiliar person were asked to describe my ethnic identity, Option A would probably be "generic white guy."

But this Sam1 had aged or decomposed in such a way as to appear Irish as hell. Age brings out the stereotypical Irishman in most Irish men. His face had brightened to a near-crimson hue. His hair had gone white. A great deal of it emerged from his nostrils and even more from his ears. I shook my head at this. Even in my most slovenly weeks and months I'd made every effort to trim my nose hair. He'd gone bald on the crown of his head. Worse, the upper half of his face was covered in half-healed scabs. It looked like most of the scabs had been freshly picked if not punched off.

Otherwise it was me alright. Same freckle by the left eye. Same nose. Same sneering, epicene lips. The only differences outside of abrasions and white hair were bigger bags under his eyes and an extra twenty years of age and anger weighing down the face, plus the type of gut that doesn't do an otherwise skinny guy any favours.

His fingernails were a bloody mess. I'd always had a nervous nail biting habit, and too often I'd woken with them chewed almost to the cuticle, red and raw. My own habit had been slowly progressing with each passing year, but I never envisioned the bloody stump stage this poor man had reached.

"Sam McQuiggan," he introduced himself, looking pretty smug about it too.

"I am fucking fully aware of that," I said.

"You are?"

"John Titor emailed me."

"What is John Titor doing here?"

"You guys screwed up, is the gist. A decade later they've got government bodies trying to fix the damage you did to the world."

"Let's get a drink," Sam1 said.

I called in sick.

"Drinks at my condo or in a bar?"

"I've been burning through a lot of cash," said Sam1.

"How much did they start you out with?"

"Ten grand."

"What's your…mission?"

"It's only a trial run. I have to bring back a newspaper."

"That's stupid," I said.

"They have to iron out the bugs before sending someone back for the important stuff."

"Were you not among the best and brightest? Expendable?" I asked, and then felt cruel.

"We come from the same stock bud, the very same stock, minus minor divergence issues."

As many have remarked, it's always trouble when a Canadian starts calling you 'bud.'

"If I get hit by a car, do you just disappear?" I asked.

"Oh man, couldn't the big hotshot John Titor have at the very least instructed you on the Everett-Wheeler model?" said Sam1.

"He sent me some links," I said, feeling oddly defensive of John Titor/Chuck.

"And you didn't read them?"

"Your tone serves as a strong indicator of why people have historically not enjoyed my company," I said.

"We aren't off to a very good start," he said. "Let's get that drink."

In my condo I poured us each a three-ounce drink. Sam2 reclined on the couch.

"A vodka-soda man," said Sam2, "No divergence there."

I described the girls. At first I glossed over the more lurid details but then figured there was no sense hiding from one's own self.

"They warned us something like that might happen to our D.O.'s. Said the odds were lower than 0.05% though. Damn. Sorry kid."

"Where's your time machine?" I asked him.

"It's in Etobicoke."

"It's in Etobicoke," I said.

"Yeah, in a van, parked at the motel room I rented."

"Why did you rent a motel in Etobicoke?"

"They have to plot a course, right? Otherwise you end up in the middle of outer space," said Sam1.

"Again, why Etobicoke?"

"Pretty close, accessible by TTC," said Sam1.

"A joke-teller," I said, sipping at my drink. "Listen joke-teller. I'd like to see this time machine."

"It takes an hour by TTC," he said.

"I can pay for a friggin' cab," I said, and cringed at the northern Ontario sound of the word *friggin'*. It had always been my sense that northern Ontario ex-pats often revert to its dialect in the company of their regional kinsmen.

The Nalgene bottle we passed back and forth drew suspicious looks from the cab driver. Otherwise it was a pleasant ride. I felt an odd comfort around Sam1, something like what twins must experience. Parked outside a Days Inn was a white Econoline van. In the rear was a rectangular box about the size of a couch.

"There it is," he said, "The TMI Sony Gravity Distortion Unit. A beaut eh?"

I whistled through my teeth, affecting the demeanour of male mechanical enthusiasm that I'd found necessary to get by in L-S-C. "How's she work?"

"There's the electron injection manifold, x-ray venting, gravity sensors, that's your six atomic clocks right there, the CPUs, all powered by two top-spin singularities that produce your run-of-the-mill off-set Tipler sinusoid," said Sam1.

"What's next for you? After you bring back the newspaper?"

"Before I bring anything back I get mine. That's the carrot, see. One trip for them and one trip for me to 2004. Did you smash those plates?"

"I did," I said.

"I'm hoping the guy in whatever 2004 I end up in smashed them too."

"Why?"

"Every reality plays out in the superverse. Somewhere Brittany Spears is the Prime Minister of England. Somewhere Sam McQuiggan happily married Nicole Esposito. You'll learn that when you read those links. But the worldlines we can safely travel to have a low divergence by necessity."

He made the first prolonged eye contact of our time together.

"If I can make it so that one Sam doesn't lose Bethany," he paused, "Then my life won't have been such a stupid waste."

"You'll just mess things up for them too," I said.

"Then I'll go just to see her face," he said petulantly.

After raising my two-litre Nalgene bottle to him in sardonic tribute, I searched for a nearby LCBO on my phone. We decided on Scotch due to a lack of mix options and resumed drinking in his motel room where he caught me up on what had transpired for him between the years of 2016 and 2037. It was enough to make me hope for maximum divergence in the years to come.

"How will you get to 2004?" I asked.

"Plotting is the one thing they taught us pretty well. It won't be the exact same worldline, like I said, but it will be almost impossible to tell the difference. I'm surprised this one is so screwed up to be honest."

"Could your handlers stop you from making multiple trips?"

"The system is designed to let us jump around as much as necessary in case we get lost. There'd be hell to pay when I got back though," said Sam1.

"How much weight can your unit handle?"

"Three-hundred pounds."

"How much do you weigh?" I asked.

"One-hundred-and-eighty pounds."

"Geez Sam1."

Something of a bean pole, I had always weighed one-fifty, even during my worst drinking years. The additional thirty pounds existed exclusively in and around Sam1's abdomen. The lesson here was that metabolism one day fails us all.

Sam1 performed a single sit-up for comedic effect.

"I'd like to go back with you," I said, "But not to 2004, instead we go back to the L-S-C of our high school years, 2001, say. There's work to be done there too."

"I don't know," said Sam1.

"You messed up my worldline. You owe me."

He sipped, pondered, and then said, "I wouldn't mind a shot at the Nicole Esposito manifested here. I never got over that little vixen. Did you play that spin the bottle game? Did you dance with her on that porch?"

"No way. I am not pimping out Nicole Esposito's dream-like physical manifestation. That is where I draw the line," I said.

"Then I'll be on my merry way. Maybe you can grab me a newspaper at the front desk?"

We continued drinking in silent stalemate. After several hours we'd hashed out a deal. I would set him up with Leslie Syrup. He would bring me back to 2001, a year we mutually considered to be at the crux of our psycho-spiritual quandary.

Before that could happen we had to lose a collective thirty pounds. Since I had very little body fat it would be damn near impossible for me to lose even ten pounds, but Sam1 said there was no way he was losing thirty, and that I'd have to meet him halfway.

We slept a few hours and then took a cab back to my condo. Lacking rubbing alcohol or Neosporin or anything, I dabbed at Sam1's facial wounds with vodka poured onto a Kleenex, causing him to scream at me. I outfitted Sam1 with sweat pants and took him to an alternate Good Feels location.

They had bought up all the competition and in some cases there were two franchises right across the street from each other. We enjoyed a thirty-minute steam. Sam1 ran on the treadmill for less than three minutes before becoming winded and near the point of collapse.

"You probably shouldn't eat anything today," I said.

"Good one," he said, "I've been thinking about McDonalds. You can't get McDonalds anymore where I'm from. All that shit is poison."

"So why do you want it?"

"Same reason you want it. It tastes good," said Sam1.

"It's mostly the salt," I said. "There's more than a gram of salt in most of the burgers. Picture a gram bag of cocaine, but full of salt, and imagine pouring that much salt on anything and how awful it would taste, but the burgers must taste so bad to begin with that they absorb all that salt and make the burger taste something like normal."

"Yeah, the salt," Sam1 said.

After a second steam we went to McDonalds. There was something fishy in that all of these Good Feels locations were surrounded by the worst fast food outlets imaginable. Either it was a conspiracy by the fast food companies to ensnare hungry people after workouts, or it was a conspiracy by the gym to ensnare fat people in the throes of post-value meal guilt. We both got McNugget meals with two barbecue sauces and one sweet and sour, diet cokes, and quarter pounders with extra pickles. We both added extra ketchup to our quarter pounders.

"You need the extra ketchup," said Sam1, "Because otherwise it's too dry."

"Yeah, but I hate looking at the patty and realizing how shit it is," I said.

"Same," said Sam1.

I raised my burger at him in a toast. The McDonalds lethargy set in before I was even halfway through my dining experience.

"If we're going to cut that weight this has to be the last meal like this. And no more drinking," I said.

"Or, if we do drink, just straight alcohol, no mix," said Sam1.

"I'm going to say no drinking period."

He nodded and then took my last two McNuggets.

"So golden," he said, "I don't care how fake it is. Nothing is this golden in 2036."

He wasn't feeling a return to Etobicoke and asked to sleep on my couch, where he immediately collapsed from a combination of exhaustion and post-McDonalds fatigue. It was just before noon, giving me plenty of time before work to Google crash diets. The two most promising were grapefruit-only and cabbage soup-only. I went down to Metro and bought twenty grapefruits and the ingredients for a bare-bones cabbage soup.

"No plans for the day?" I asked Sam1. "You don't want to experience some 2016 culture?"

"I remember 2016. Not much I'm interested in experiencing again," he said.

"I need to sleep for a while before work," I said, "Try not to burn the place down."

When I woke up the soup smelled excellent. Before I could pour myself a bowl I saw Sam1 lying face down on the floor. I nudged at his ribs with my foot. I cursed myself for not dispensing with the latest sixty I'd bought.

"Sam1, what I need from you here is a commitment. What you might call 'buy-in.'"

"Thought I could mix the vodka with the grapefruit

juice," he slurred, and then brightened, "I ate three of the damn things."

"I did notice the crudely-mashed grapefruits on the counter, Sam1."

I put a bowl of soup in front of him. "Eat that," I said, "You'll need the energy. You are going to work out for the entirety of my eight hour shift."

"Hell."

I threw a garbage bag at him. "You'll wear this."

When Randy saw us enter Good Feels he gasped.

"Your father?" he asked. "Strong family resemblance."

Why not?

"Yep, this is the old man. He is rededicating himself to fitness."

"Personal honour to meet you," said Randy.

I hit Quick Start on a treadmill and set it for 3mph/10 incline. "We're going for endurance here Sam1."

"Eat a dick," said Sam1.

I was nervous the entire shift, certain that Nicole and Sherilyn would show up, and even more certain Sam1 would embarrass me somehow. After my break I was unpleasantly surprised to see Alicia Principe. Sam1 was repositioned by the squat rack to best observe the fruits of her treadmill work. He gave me a big lecherous wink. I grabbed him by the collar of the t-shirt and hauled him over to the kiosk.

"Please do not manhandle me, young man," he said.

"That could be the real Alicia Principe," I said, "She's a fitness model in Toronto now."

"You know it probably isn't," Sam1 said.

My monitor revealed an account with the dubious hyphenated name of Alicia Queen-Fohraday.

"Okay, so it's not her. How do I proceed?" asked Sam1,

shoulders hunched, a shifty old codger.

Forgive me a moment of direct address: try to envision yourself at your most indecent, somehow external and observable to you, but then also at least 15x worse. What's so terrible about being a perv, I realized, is that you never stop being a perv, even when you're old, arthritic, hair emerging from every orifice, unappealing to all but the most damaged fetishists.

When I didn't answer he left and spoke to her at the treadmill. He returned deflated and gave me a look. I sighed and walked over to Alicia Principe/Queen-Fohraday. "Please continue working out until 8 am. Don't overtax yourself and be sure to drink a lot of water."

"Doesn't she invoke any feeling in you?" Sam1 asked a moment later, "Don't you remember our nineteenth birthday?"

"I remember passing out around midnight at my birthday party," I said.

"I didn't pass out. I made out with her at The Handshake Room."

I was impressed. As must have been the patrons of The Handshake Room, a nickname I'd given to L-S-C's lone nightclub, The Ace of Spades, because all anyone ever did there was shake hands and pat the same thirty or so people on the back. Alicia Principe was a 9/10. I had just grown into my adult looks in 2002, a golden window of time when my stock had been on the rise. Alicia would have been the perfect girl to elevate my status during that period, as she'd gone to a school on the other side of the city, and hadn't known me in the literal lean years (115 pounds) between 1998 and 2001. Assuming Sam1 had endured the same scarcity of sexual attentions, those moments of proximity to Alicia Principe must have carried emotional weight for him.

"But she'd been drunk, and denied it the next day, while I told everyone I could, so pretty pathetic and embarrassing, all things considered," continued Sam1.

"We are sick people, Sam1. We are sexually unwell. We are motivated by ancient slightings."

"Can I have more soup?" he asked.

"If you have soup now you'll have nothing to eat for the next six hours," I told him.

A sneer of dejection led Sam1 back to his treadmill. When I walked past, the machine was on 1.5 mph and 0 incline, known by some in the fitness community as *barely moving*. I decided to pick my battles.

Three hours later Nicole and Sherilyn came in. I swiped their cards and turned to see if Sam1 had noticed. He was nowhere to be seen. I found him in the change room, drinking from a mysterious water bottle.

"Secret water bottles eh?" I said.

He made a sound indicative of refreshment and passed the bottle my way. I took a whiff. It was either Isopropyl alcohol from the hand sanitizer unit diluted with water or straight vodka. Not noticing any of the tell-tale soap bubbles, I deemed it safe to drink.

We passed it back and forth a few times before I said, "They're here."

"Who?"

"You know who. I'd like to get this whole deal behind us. How do I know you won't give me the slip after?"

"You'll have to trust me," said Sam1.

"If you can't trust an alternate version of yourself from an alternate version of your own future then who can you trust? I believe that's how the saying goes," I said.

At the front desk Randy gave me a suspicious look.

"I mean no offense with question," said Randy, "Drinking on work property? Bad influence of derelict father?"

"Not the case, Randy," I said, "Had a little accident with the hand sanitizer in the change room. Isopropyl everywhere."

"Even in direction of mouth, originating spot of smell?"

"Afraid so."

"Major relief to me. Apologies for mistrustful accusation," said Randy.

"No harm done Randy. I admire your vigilance."

I visited Sam1 at his treadmill.

"Let's get this over with," I said, "Who's the lucky gal?"

He took a moment to admire the three girls. "You've brought back two. Why should I have to choose?"

I pursed my lips and tapped them a bunch of times with my left index finger.

"This will be the last and only time?" I asked.

"You have my word," said Sam1.

"My own personal word is worth little, but okay."

When it was time to go I took Nicole and Alicia on my arm, and nodded at Sherilyn to follow. An unfortunate analogy came to mind—the idea of having three dogs but only two leashes, and leaving the most loyal dog unleashed hoping he'd follow the pack. When Sam1 tried to take Sherilyn's arm she pulled away in revulsion. He looked at me, hurt.

In my lobby the concierge's brows communicated suspicion. Seeing me with a pretty girl or two was one thing. Seeing me with three plus a coarsened look-a-like was another.

"Hey Marty, this is my father. He's staying with me for a few days," I said.

It was a tough sell. Though he'd lived a hard life, Sam1 possessed the drunkard's youthful élan. Maybe older brother would have been the better story. But then in the history of human genealogy no twin brothers have been born twenty years apart.

Upstairs Sam1 poured drinks and tried to sidle up to each girl. Sherilyn leaned as far away as she could from him. Nicole closed her eyes. Alicia held her hand up in the classic, "Talk to the hand cause the face don't wanna hear it" position.

Sam2 took me into the bedroom. "Whatever motivates these figures, it starts with you," he said, "You'll have to give them some hypnotic suggestion to love me."

"Here's the thing, Sam1, they have not loved me. I do not believe they are capable of love. They have been at best complacent."

He laced his hands behind his head. "Then give them the complacency directive."

This really was going too far. I could only imagine the retribution forthcoming from the legion of John Titors. But I was desperate for whatever approximation of my L-S-C youth Sam1's machine could afford me. That was the place and time I couldn't escape. I needed resolution there and then. I rationalized that the girls in my living room were manifestations free of consciousness, nothing but sacks of skin chanced upon in dreams. In the living room I said to each girl, "You will remain complacent with Sam1. You will feel no emotion towards him one way or another. If you are somehow real, you will have no recollection of this." I paused. "Sam1 is the older guy in the next room."

"Have fun," I told him, weary and disgusted. "I'll be drinking heavily in my room and watching *Total Divas* with the headphones in."

Halfway into my first episode the sugared-ozone smell of crack cocaine wafted under my bedroom door. I emerged liked a tired parent.

"Where and when did you get crack?" I asked.

"The same place we've always gotten crack is where, and last evening while you were sleeping is when," said Sam1.

During my heavy drinking years I would occasionally stumble down George Street and buy a $20 stone. For me it was no more addictive than regular cocaine, and could keep me going. It's a miracle I never got my head caved in as I'd weaved around the most dangerous street in Toronto yelling at recent occupants of the Don Jail over short counts.

"Give me a blast at least," I said.

He packed about a five dollar chunk into a marijuana pipe he also must have bought the previous night. This was wasteful, but I was glad not to have a crack pipe in my home. That crossed a line, somehow. The in uteran safety of freebase cocaine sealed itself around me. I closed my eyes and experienced internal bliss. Crack is a sad substance. Those first few times feel better than winning the Super Bowl. So why risk the concussions and put in all those years of practise when it's right there on the street corner? I smiled and shook my head and squeezed Sam1's neck. I got on my knees in front of Nicole and said, "I loved you so much Nicole, don't you know that? Why couldn't you love me back?"

"I don't know," she said.

At that moment the crack euphoria descended into its doom-y inevitability, the average upswing of a crack blast being about fifteen seconds in my experience, whereas I'd imagine the Super Bowl high lasts at least a day or two.

"God, you are so disgusting Sam1." I said, "Is this the best you can aspire to? You might as well be stroking a blow-up doll. And how does it help? How does it fix whatever went wrong with us?"

"Don't you moralize with me, punk. You made these

girls. They wouldn't be here if you didn't want them to be. You're sicker than me. I am an innocent time traveler in this scenario. TMI industries did not say word one regarding this type of baloney," said Sam1.

We stood up in classic L-S-C menace mode and I cracked him in the jaw. It was a pathetic scene with lots of fumbling and grappling, concluded only when I manoeuvred him into a de facto hip toss through my glass coffee table.

"Jesus, the neighbours are going to complain," I said.

We got paranoid. We herded the girls into my room. We sprayed air freshener to cover up the smell of crack. Both of us cut our hands trying to get the broken glass into garbage bags.

"Why man?" I asked him, "Why are we so fucked?"

He took a drink. I took a drink from his glass. He gave me a hug.

"We'll get through this Sam2," he said, for the first time seeming like the older and wiser Sam, "We'll go back and we'll do some good."

I sat down and tapped my foot at a rate of about five taps per second.

"You know I'm still going to do this," he said.

I lacked the strength to argue. He smoked crack again and blew the smoke out of my kitchen window, which was considerate of him. He went in the bedroom. I plugged my headphones into the TV to block out his noises. When he was done he came out looking guilty and sad.

"This was a bad idea," he said.

"Kind of like people who are into femdom," I said, also having smoked more crack while he was in the bedroom. "It seems like a great idea and then you ejaculate and there you are with a ball in your mouth and cum inside your male chastity belt thing seeping back into your urethra and probably causing infection."

"You've got to wonder how Jeffrey Dahmer felt after he came like in the mouth of a skull or whatever? Like here I am, I Jeffrey Dahmer have killed this human being to have his skull so I could come in it, and now I've came, and where has it gotten me?" added Sam1.

"Upswings and downswings in perviness must afflict and haunt all pervs," I said. "Just as even the most puritanical masturbator loses his interest, in, oh let's say, breasts, after the act is culminated and his browser history deleted."

"I bet the worst perv, the guy wearing a diaper, rolling around in broken glass, a goddamn dungeon full of prisoners beneath him, is pure at heart in his finer moments," said Sam1.

"Yeah, and then while wiping up he's like 'Why do I have all these school children confined in this dungeon?' and he struggles to remember what even caused him to construct a dungeon in the first place," I said.

"Then he thinks of releasing them from the dungeon but of course can't, so it all leads to grim death. Curse the human libido!" said Sam1.

"I'd say curse the male libido. The female libido doesn't seem to have such a destructive bent to it," I said.

Sam1 ruminated on that.

"I'll see the girls out now," I said.

I led them downstairs. "Go on," I said, shooing them away like racoons, "Back to where you came from."

Then some vestigial crack dopamine produced in me a weird whimsy, and I crooned, "Someday soon, we'll meet again, don't know where, don't know when," and then added in a speaking tone, "And don't have me prosecuted for aiding and abetting in cosmic sex crimes against you, please ladies."

••••• **13** •••••

Sleep didn't come easy and required so much lubrication that I had to send Sam1 out with my credit card for more booze. At 8 pm I logged into Nicole's Facebook. There was a message to Sherilyn.

Nicole: Oh God, Oh God, Oh God, Oh God, Oh God, Oh God, Oh God, Oh God.

Sherilyn: I know, I know, I know, I know, I know, I know, I know.

There was also a message from Alicia Principe to which Nicole had not responded.

Alicia: I had the weirdest dream about you and Sherilyn.

On our walk to Good Feels Sam1 and I made all sorts of vows. He surprised me by asking if he could confess at St. James Cathedral after the eight-hour work/workout shift. Apparently he'd become a born-again Christian, partially after his second AA stint, and then full-fledged and fanatical after his first NA stint, and finally back to what he considered a healthy median position after his third AA stint.

I won't dwell on the details of the days that followed. We tried to straighten out and fly right. Picture a *Rocky* movie montage: Sams hitting treadmills, consuming cabbage soup, Sam1 praying to his God in the cathedral, a lot of farting. Syrup came to the door of Good Feels one day and I straight up turned her away. I hope the real Nicole appreciates that.

Sam1 was losing about a half pound a week. At that rate it would take months, and his presence in the condo was beginning to cramp my style, even though technically we shared a personal style. Sometimes he would pee on the toilet seat for example, which I also do, but one's own pee is largely inoffensive. I took to Google to look for better weight-loss methods. In under a minute I found one that made me feel like an idiot for not looking harder the first time. Such is the fuckery and false confidence borne of ever-immediate information! A bodybuilding message board detailed how fighters cut weight before weigh-ins using a "flushing mode." It called on us to follow this water drinking schedule.

> Day 1 – 2 — gallons
> Day 2 – 1 — gallon
> Day 3 – 1 — gallon
> Day 4 – .5 — gallons
> Day 5 – .25 — gallons
> Day of Departure – No water till arrival at destination at 2 am.

We could only eat fifty grams of carbs a day but as much fatty meat as we wanted. Hot baths were for some reason imperative. So were saunas on the final days but not on the initial ones. We aimed to drop a combined forty pounds and use the extra ten pounds for clothing, money, and identification.

Sam1 had legit ID that appeared to have been issued in 1998. I didn't have any, but fortunately had one of those old white and red health cards that don't require renewal. I withdrew my liquid assets and stuffed my wallet with $100 bills after going from bank to bank asking for old bills. There weren't a lot of fifteen-year-old hundreds in circulation, so the day before our departure I got desperate and ended up paying a huge premium to an antique currency salesman on eBay.

It wasn't clear what would happen to the equity in my apartment. Sam1 could get me back to a worldline less than five decimal places of divergence removed from the one we were leaving, where the condo should have been waiting upon my return, but nothing was certain. In a worst case scenario I'd return to a worldline in which yet another Sam occupied my condo and the deed belonged to him.

I wanted to query John Titor/Chuck on the matter, but knew he'd put the kibosh on our plans in no time. We were lucky he hadn't cracked down on us already. Knowing as narrator how this narrative ends, let me say I would have been way better off had John Titor stopped us right then, in 2016, before I could commit what World Governments yet unforeseeable would consider capital crimes against temporality.

Sam1 determined that February 18th would be the most favourable jump window for months. He plotted the details of where we'd land in L-S-C using Google Earth. I suggested Mount Trashmore, an L-S-C sledding hill built on a mountain of trash. But Sam1 said the incline could cause the Econoline to land haphazardly and send us tumbling to deaths by neck-breaking, a bad way to go. The only space large and open enough was Bellamy Field.

On day three of our flush-out Sam1 asked me a question over our steak, ground beef and bun-less hot dog supper. "Can I see Nicole one last time?"

"Dude, why?"

"I've always missed her."

"We're creatures of sentiment," I said, and sighed. "I believe she will have to be considered, thunk of that is, to be manifested. This will be taxing for me. Can't you see her when we get to L-S-C?"

"You recommend that a fifty-one-year-old man accost a

seventeen-year-old cherubic type on the streets of L-S-C, and not months removed from the D'Agostino sex abuse scandal?"

"Fine. But if you want me to think of her then you too must think of her."

We sat and shared our recollections of the girl. The hours spent in her lavish home watching movies. Her big white dog Bingo. Her little smile and laugh. The time she'd visited unexpectedly, right at the onset of our new adult appearance, and shrieked, "You look so cute." The time we'd danced drunkenly with her on the back porch at a party, and the following day when our confession that it had 'meant so much' to us had been greeted by her claim that she did not remember the experience.

That night at the gym Randy said, "Great deal of sudden weight loss. Father is unimpeachable influence on health."

"Listen Randy, I may have to accompany my father out of the province for a while. It's not decided yet, but I could be gone for some time."

Randy touched my shoulder and said, "You are my greatest friend in Canadian life."

"Thanks Randy," I said, "You've been my greatest friend also."

"If not returning I will keep memories of you in my heart."

"I'll remember you in my heart too."

We exchanged awkward pats on the back.

Sam1 gave up on exercise once our flushing regiment appeared to be working, but he was hanging around the gym to keep temptation at bay. In came Leslie Syrup.

"What should I say to her?" he asked.

"This is for me to come up with? You wanted her here. You foisted unwanted considerations upon me. You better have something plenty poignant to say," I said.

He got halfway to her before doing an about-face. "Almost forgot. You better give her the hypnotic suggestion first," he said, "Or she'll be repulsed."

I went to her and said, "Please hear out what Sam1 has to say." I paused, and pointed, "That's that guy."

Sam1 took her hand and looked her in the eyes. "I know it's all meaningless, just a high school crush, but I have dreams where we're giving each other hugs. There must be some place for that affection to go that isn't creepy and weird. Can you just acknowledge that it exists and that you're cool with it?"

She stared straight into him, but I might have seen a sparkle of recognition in her eyes.

"We had some good times together. You used to laugh. You used to giggle and say, 'You're so funny,' when I said something funny," said Sam1.

"You used to be pretty funny, yeah," said Leslie Syrup.

He smiled, only his lips conveying happiness.

"Bye Nicole. Sorry for the other night," he said.

He walked away. She still stood there, so I went over and said, "You can resume exercising now, or go home. You don't ever have to come back."

⸱⸱⸱ 14 ⸱⸱⸱

On the night of the launch it was -21 degrees Celsius but felt like -27. The van wouldn't start when we arrived. It didn't need to be on for the Temporal Distortion Unit to work, but we wanted the heat. Against Sam1's better discretion we got a boost from another patron of the hotel and after a few minutes the van was nice and toasty.

Sam1 had plotted the journey in advance, and was making some final administrations to his unit's dashboard. I checked my phone to try and feel important.

"Heavy snowfall in L-S-C," I said. "Will that be a factor?"

"That's on this worldline. And anyway the whole thing has more to do with gravitic tidal forces," said Sam1.

"Yeah," I said.

"We're ready. Step inside Sam2."

"Step inside? I thought we sat in the van," I said.

"Nope."

"Then how did the van get here?"

"The machine transports everything within the van's radius, but it's not safe for us humans."

"But John Titor sat in his car. John Titor's machine was only the size of a suitcase."

"I guess your hero John Titor had things figured out just a bit better. Don't you think TMI studied the John Titor story down to the smallest detail? This, Sam2, is the best we can do."

I held out my palms in the universal "ease up" gesture.

The TDU didn't have seats, more like one groove meant for one person.

"Where do I sit?" I asked.

"You'll have to sit on my lap."

"Good one."

He wasn't joking, so I sat on his lap.

"You better not get a boner," I said.

"You'd probably like it," he said.

It was pretty ridiculous, impugning the heterosexuality of your own alternate self like that. This was how deeply ingrained facetious homosexuality was in your L-S-C-born male. He handed me a pair of cheap sunglasses.

"Put these on," he said, "Ultraviolet radiation."

This early-model Sony TDU travelled one year per hour. Our temporal destination of 2001 would take fourteen hours. The gravity field pulled at our guts like a roller coaster feeling. I was glad to have nothing in my stomach. Outside of a faint hum and the sound of static electricity popping there was no external stimulus. It was like being in a sensory deprivation tank, something I'd later do with the naturopath Dr. Jessica Rittle. We were both hungry and thirsty as devils. I was constantly shifting to try and get into a more comfortable position.

"If you keep moving around on me I seriously am going to get a boner," said Sam1, "Strictly from friction, but that's a psychological can of worms I have no interest in opening."

"It would give new meaning to terms like *onanism* and *self-gratification,*" I said.

"Seriously, this is getting weird," said Sam1.

When the unit's monitor ticked down to zero there was nothing to do but pop our heads out like prairie dogs and hope to see Bellamy Park.

We didn't. The first thing I saw through the van's tinted window was the hot dog cart that positioned itself outside The Handshake Room on Friday and Saturday nights. The second thing was Dave Reid, not yet nineteen, but with a fake ID like all the popular kids, standing in line and shivering in a t-shirt, though the temperature on this worldline was also in the -20s. I wanted to go pat him on the back or something. Reconcile like dream-night Sam always needed to do. Say, "How's it been going pal?"

"What now?" I asked Sam1.

"We get the hell out of here."

Sam1 got behind the wheel and sped down King Street.

Five minutes later he parked at Bellamy Field and ran to the van's rear.

"What's going on?" I asked.

"I have these license stickers," he said, and showed me stickers for 1994, 1998, 2001, 2004, right up until 2028. "They can't be older than three years old and they can't be from the future, or we'd get pulled over."

It was obvious he should have put these on in the moments preceding our departure, but I didn't want to be a Monday morning quarterback regarding Sam1's time travel logistics.

"Why would they give you those?"

"In case I got lost."

"Are we lost?"

"That sure looked like 2001-era Dave Reid to me," said Sam1.

He consulted the readouts on his machine and said, "That's weird. Exactly double the divergence. The divergence on your worldline was 1.4% from my original one. The divergence on this worldline is 2.8% from the one we just left. 2.8 isn't bad though. We can deal with 2.8."

"I'm starving," I said.

"Me too, but if memory serves even the fast food places close at nine in this dump."

"Not true. Don't you remember the Christmas Eve dinners at The Husky?"

Among my (our) circle(s) of friends it had been a high school tradition to spend Christmas Eve not at Christmas mass, nor around hearth and home, but in the worst dive diner in the region. We'd order beef stroganoff and chicken parm and feel somehow exceptional. Sometimes we'd throw a football across the highway for added ridiculousness. This kind of self-conscious irony is prized in places with precious little to do just as it is universally prized among the dull.

A familiar ache came over me as we drove down L-S-C's main drag. After my first semester in Toronto, that first visit home, that first reunion with the only place I'd known—how perfect the place had seemed. That night at The Upstairs Bar I'd given a rousing speech, and my gang from the time had put our hands in on a vow to live in L-S-C's simple confines forever, drinking six packs on the golf course and shaking hands at whatever adult bar would go on to supplant The Handshake Room. But on each subsequent visit L-S-C began to seem a little more small time, a little bit shittier. I'd had no means of measuring whether L-S-C was actually getting worse, or if big city life had simply spoiled the place for me.

In the early years after my departure all the people I'd loved in my life belonged there and I no longer did. Yet those who continued to belong in L-S-C all yearned for anything external to L-S-C, and must have envied my big city life. So I could never tell if L-S-C had cuckolded me, by hanging on to my old friends and providing a womb of camaraderie for them even in my absence, or if I'd cuck'd it with Toronto. Now, with the benefit of a Temporal Distortion Unit, even as I experienced that familiar L-S-C melancholia, I was for the first time certain that L-S-C had always kind of sucked.

"L-S-C, you old heartbreaker," I said with a mix of sarcasm and genuine affection, and then asked Sam1, "When was the last time you came back?"

"Dad's funeral," he said.

"Me too."

We were tired of proteins. Proteins no longer held appeal for us. We ordered poutines with extra cheese. We drank glass after glass of mildew-smelling water. After our first round of entrees Sam1 ordered ravioli and I ordered fettuccine alfredo and we shared the meals family style.

"It is dawning on me," said Sam1, "That we have not done much planning."

"I was hoping you'd been planning but had failed to mention your plans," I said.

"Afraid not. What comes to mind is shelter."

"Hotel room?" I asked.

"The thing about that," said Sam1, "Is while my credit card looks real, if swiped it won't be linked to any credit agency."

"Do they actually check your card when you pay cash at a motel, or do they just hold the number in case you wreck the room?" I asked.

"No idea," said Sam1.

"This is exactly the type of thing I would have Googled on my phone."

"Yeah, now we'd have to wait for an internet café to open."

"The past is so shit," I said.

I went outside to stretch my legs. I asked a trucker filling his tank about the row of trucks parked out back. He told me that the truckers paid fifteen dollars to park overnight and enjoy the shower facilities, and so long as the lot wasn't full, and Barb was in a good mood, that she might let us park our van there. After a twenty-five percent tip Barb accepted our proposal. She was adamant that we not shower though, claiming the truckers wouldn't tolerate non-truckers in their showers. I didn't argue, but at first I thought, 'Wouldn't non-truckers generally be in a state of better hygiene than someone who'd been on the road for days?' Then I realized that any non-trucker so hard up as to need a Husky shower was probably a lice-ridden hobo.

The Husky had a little store attached to it and we bought blankets, L-S-C "Catch the Excitement" sweatshirts, and two microwavable heat packs that Barb was kind enough to microwave for us. There wasn't much room to lie down in the van because of the TDU, but so long as we lay perfectly straight it was tolerable.

"Catch the excitement," I said. "In my day we used to say, 'Catch the excrement.'"

"Let's talk big picture," said Sam1.

"Okay. We're here to fix the rift, whatever went wrong in us when Dave Reid abdicated his friendship responsibilities," I said.

"There's two ways to approach this," said Sam1, "Either we get hold of Sam3 and start counselling him, build up his confidence, tell him Dave Reid isn't so important, that he Sam3 will go on to big things, and maybe by doing that we save this Sam."

"What's the other option?"

"We kill Dave Reid," said Sam1.

The extra fifteen years of dark living had brought Sam1 to the point where he could not just kill, but kill an alternate version of a friend he'd once loved. I was more saddened than shocked.

"What does that accomplish?" I asked.

"It's 2001, right? Meaning Dave Reid only pulled away from us in the last several months. If he dies now, there's a big memorial service, everyone remembers he used to be close to Sam3, Sam3 is ratified as a minor hero for losing his close friend, and boom, he goes on to a happy and healthy life," said Sam1.

"Let me meet you in the middle here. We kidnap Dave

Reid and reason with him. Tell him how sad he's making Sam3. Dave Reid, who I guess we need to be calling Dave2, is not without compassion."

"He should actually be Dave3. Because to me, there's a Dave Reid back on your worldline, and he's Dave2, even though he didn't factor into the narrative. Anyway, let's table that for the time being. We have more immediate issues to consider. First we need lodging. Let's look in the paper tomorrow, find a scummy-looking place to sublet, offer a bunch of cash in advance."

"Good thinking," I said.

"The bigger problem is this van. Can you imagine the reaction of Sam3's parents or Dave Reid3's when this giant rape-mobile is parked outside their house for any period of time? Not to mention it just mysteriously appeared out of nowhere outside L-S-C's most popular bar."

"Can't we buy a less ridiculous car with cash?" I asked.

"We have to watch our cash," said Sam1, "Unless you want to start bussing tables for under the table pay while we're here."

My eyes widened. "It's Friday, February 1st. You know what's coming up? Superbowl 36. The Patriots over The Rams."

"There's the 2.8% divergence to consider," said Sam1.

"I'm no pro gambler, but a 97% chance at victory seems like a risk worth taking."

"I swore oaths about that kind of thing," said Sam1.

It struck me as a little late in the game for oath-keeping, but I said nothing.

The next morning we woke surly, as we so often did. Since we both found coffee neurotoxic there was nothing to do but slowly ease into the day. It would be a challenging one, the type that coffee was made for. Neurochemical intolerance to caffeine is one of life's cruellest curses. I can't overstate that.

Our taste for protein was back and we each enjoyed a double order of crispy bacon. Sam1 returned to our table with a copy of the L-S-C Courier. On the front page, above the fold, was Brent Steiner's column, an L-S-C Courier institution dedicated to animal hijinx, municipal political hand-wringing, and very rare stories of the Fortean or inexplicable. The gigantic photo of our van beneath the fold indicated this column belonged in the latter category. The copy read:

Is someone in L-S-C on a Magical Mystery Tour?

No, the Fab 4 from Liverpool didn't stop by The Ace of Spades last night, but a mysterious van sure did.

Patrons in line for the popular King Street bar claim that the full-sized Econoline van pictured below simply materialized from out of nowhere before speeding off.

Say what?

"I happened to be looking in that direction, and for real, this van just…appeared," said Anthony Spadafore, 19. "Weirdest thing I ever saw in my life. No word of a lie."

Well, this columnist would never accuse a prominent Junior A hockey player like Spadafore of deceit, but these folks were in line for a bar after all, so Occam's Razor, the most logical explanation is that someone's eyes played tricks on them and an incident of mass hysteria followed.

If you or someone you know is the owner of this van I'd love to hear from you.

Brent Steiner would be the lone reporter left at the Courier by my last visit in 2015. But in 2002 he was one of ten, so it surprised me that this unsubstantiated story would be the day's biggest news. Then I looked at the other front page stories and remembered that there just wasn't very much news in L-S-C.

"Not off to a great start, anonymity-wise," I said to Sam1.

"Shit no."

We browsed the classifieds and circled three listings in the lowest income areas of town.

"Roommate or roommates wanted on Boar Street," said Sam1.

It was a single bedroom in a four-bedroom apartment. The rent of $100 a month was low even by L-S-C standards circa 2001. Then again, no way the rent on the whole place was $400, so we'd be subsidizing the existing tenants.

The scent of marijuana with an undercurrent of hash oil greeted us on the second floor. Steve 'Blinky' Blake opened the door, providing both a pleasant surprise and a dreary portrait of the foredoomed. The most clichéd stoner I'd met in my life, complete with white-person dreadlocks and poor dental hygiene, Blinky possessed the type of stupidity a man must work at. Though I'd shared many classes with him, and could have easily spotted a Blinky fifteen-years aged, he sure didn't recognize us.

The blighting to come was that Steve 'Blinky' Blake's marijuana enthusiasm and synchronic low earning potential ran its natural course, as he'd go on to ecstasy abuse in the mid-aughts, and then be among the hardest hit by the Purdue-perpetrated Oxy epidemic that hit full speed around 2008. When I say hardest hit I don't refer to dependence, withdrawal, and etc. I do refer to a life of crime, though jail would not be in the cards for Steve 'Blinky' Blake. He was one of the first people killed (chopped up, more like) in a series of Oxy-related murders that would wake L-S-C to the realization that they weren't in a northern Ontarian, low-crime Kansas anymore, and that Purdue had managed to ruin a tiny town on the shores of Lake Temagami, a town that surely Purdue's top strategists could not name.

"Here about the room," said Sam1.

After about thirty of his trademark blinks Blinky held out his arm in the well-known, "This is it," gesture. Then Blinky was given pause.

"It's only one room eh. You're not fags are you?"

The question was asked without malice. This was merely the cultural climate in Blinky's L-S-C. Though he'd probably never shared more than a sentence or two with an openly gay person, as a heterosexual living with two other bros he could not be responsible for bringing in two eerily-similar queer interlopers.

"Fuck you," said Sam1, striking the appropriate tone of good-natured but vehement denial. "No way. Just passing through town. We need a place for a month or two. You guys cool with cash?"

"Cash is king, right?" said Blinky, revealing his facility with low-level economic tropes.

"Is the room furnished?"

"There's like these mats on the ground," stated Blinky.

Sam1 held up one of our hundred dollar bills. "I think we can trust each other without a contract. Might a spare key be provided?"

"You can copy mine at the mall I guess," said Blinky.

"Superlative," said Sam1. "I noticed a red Nissan out back. Is that yours?"

"It's mine," said Blinky.

"Does it run?"

"Needs a new battery and probably some other shit."

"Blinky, we would like to rent your car. It appears you weren't using it. So how does an extra $100 a month sound?

Plus we'll replace the battery and get her running," said Sam1.

I gave Sam1 a look. Blinky had not introduced himself. I gave Blinky a look. Blinky appeared oblivious to our occulted knowledge of his name. I gave Sam1 a second look of, "I guess everything is cool because Blinky's brain is so fried."

"Whoa, where did you guys come from?" asked Blinky, "You're like solving all my problems in one go. Hey do you guys want to fire one up you know. Least I can do man. Least I can do."

"No thanks," Sam1 said.

Blinky looked pretty broken up about that, so I promised to smoke weed with him in the future.

We drove to the Central Mall in the suspicious Econo-line van hoping we wouldn't run into Brent Steiner or a loyal reader.

One memory myth was confirmed by the crowd at the Central Mall. As kids in L-S-C this 455,000 sq. foot retail mecca really had been central to our lives. It was the third largest mall in northern Ontario behind only the New Sudbury Centre and the Station Mall in Sault Ste. Marie. I'd get dropped off with Dave Reid in the eighth grade and we'd spend entire days browsing compact discs, meeting girls from other elementary schools, and feigning rebellion against the L-S-C lifestyle code we were hardwired to obey while eating slices of L-S-C's abnormally excellent pizza.

Like most of L-S-C, the Central Mall shrunk in significance once I left for Toronto. With each passing year the mall seemed sadder and smaller. With each visit home one of the major stores had been replaced with the general equivalent of a thrift shop. By 2008 half the mall was boarded up and vacant. Towards my parents' final years, based on the appearance of the typical customer, I believe the mall was used primarily for Oxy and Fentanyl deals and the commerce of tin foil, mini soldering torches, and other dragon-chasing accessories.

On this Saturday in 2001 it downright bustled. People appeared happy and industrious. L-S-C appeared to have economic meaning and vigour.

"Here is the heart of L-S-C. Here is how I want to remember the Central Mall," I said.

Sam1 sung the mall's familiar jingle, "The Central Mall, the nucleus of it all."

We bought a big battery, some rudimentary tools, two sleeping bags and two pillows. It cost us almost $200 in 2001 money.

"Let's get a slice," I said.

We went to Mrs. Vespasian's Italian Eats in the food court and got the thick-crusted, so-cheesy-as-to-negatively-affect-profits pizza that you just cannot get outside of L-S-C. Twenty-six high school girls came into the food court on their lunch break. They laughed. They smiled. Their brown skin shone with the cosmetic greases they'd applied by locker mirrors. Their collective scent overtook the foodstuffs before us.

"We better get out of here," said Sam1.

Back on Boar Street, I was impressed by how easily Sam1 got Blinky's car up and running. He explained that he'd taken a number of mechanical courses in preparation for his time travel jaunt. We smoked a joint with Blinky, ordered yet more pizza from Mrs. Vespasian's west end location, and retired to our stinking room to plot the kidnapping of Dave 'Reeder' Reid.

15

"It's Saturday evening. Where do we find him?" asked Sam1.

"Let's call his house."

"Won't that be weird?"

"No, we have the same voice," I said, my voice having dropped to a deep baritone when I was about twelve, sounding quite stupid then, and only coming to suit me in later years, if ever.

"You sound the same. I sound more grizzled," said Sam1.

We argued for fifteen minutes about how grizzled Sam1 did or did not sound before I agreed to call.

In the living room Blinky and the gang were passing a bong around. I asked their de facto leader, Big Roger, if I could use the cordless phone. Big Roger consented. The number was the only one from my L-S-C years that had not escaped me. Back in our room I hit #67 before dialling, which in this time and region could block caller display. Dave's step-mother answered the phone. She had a girlish voice I recalled as the gateway to the hour-long bullshit sessions Dave and I had shared until the unnoticeable gradient of betrayal started sloping on down in the eleventh grade.

"Sam, haven't heard from you in a while. Where have you been?" she asked.

What could I say? Abandoned, was the answer that came to mind.

"Around. What's Dave up to tonight?"

"He's got basketball until nine and then they're all going over to Marty Calcofluco's. Should I tell him you called?"

"No, it's fine."

"Alright then. Stop by sometime. We miss you around here."

She was being polite. She never gave a fuck about me.

"He's playing basketball," I told Sam1, "He never played basketball."

"Nope, soccer and football. There's our first divergence."

"Better now than during The Patriots big win," I said.

At Canadian Tire we loaded a cart with duct tape, two ski masks, and two baseball bats. Realizing the suspiciousness of this we also bought bags of chips, canned ravioli and cases of bottled water to stock our room with.

Parked down the block from Calcofluco's place, we could see the cars coming and going. Around 10:30 pm the Camaro owned and compulsively polished by Dave Reid's dad pulled up, and three indistinguishable figures got out.

"Maybe tonight's not a good night," I said.

"Nah, he'll have to drive home eventually. Then we'll get him," said Sam1.

We listened to The Otter Q98.3, one of L-S-C's two competing classic rock radio formats. There was still a country station and a pop station in 2001. By 2015 the two classic rock stations would be all that remained, waging a final existential duel with weapons called Steve Miller Band and Peter Frampton.

Sam1 handed me a mickey of vodka.

"Where did you get that?" I asked.

"When you went to the bathroom at the mall I hit the LCBO."

"Jesus," I said after a hard slam. It was warm and I almost spit it out.

"Tonight will be trying work," said Sam1, "Emotionally

and otherwise."

Dave3 drove only one friend home. The other guy must have gotten a ride from someone else. We followed at a safe distance. Sam1 was pretty good at trailing a guy, but claimed he was only having luck with the lights, and this wasn't something he'd learned in time traveler boot camp.

When Dave finally parked in his driveway we had to act fast, but were not prepared to act fast.

"Get him," cried Sam1.

We ran out and wielded the bats.

"Come with us or it won't be pretty," said Sam1.

"Sam?" asked Dave Reid3.

My voice, our voices, was/were nothing if not distinctive.

Sam1 hit him in the thigh. Easily the dumbest place to hit a person with a bat. It would only leave a bruise at best, but sure managed to anger Reeder. Reeder disarmed Sam1 with an efficacious wrist-chop, and, ever-gallant, even facing a second bat-armed opponent, tossed the bat thirty yards away. He then knocked out Sam1 with a concise hook to the left cheekbone.

I took a couple steps back.

"Put down that bat," said Dave Reid.

"I can't," I said.

"Wait, are you Sam?" he asked.

I didn't want to hit him. I sort of wanted to hit him. I thought of a hundred or so solitary nights I could have benefitted from his company on and cracked him clean in the skull like I was Paul Molitor.

Thankfully, L-S-C suburbs post-midnight are not happening places. I dragged Dave into the backseat of the car and taped the heck out of his hands. I dragged Sam1 into the car and put him in the front seat. Then I took Sam1's ski mask and put it backwards over Dave3's head and drove back to the apartment building.

We had parked the van in an alley behind the building and planned to use it as our interrogation room. Sam1, coming to just moments before Dave, decided more duct tape was in order, and used an entire role on Dave's hands and feet.

"I did not expect to be disarmed so easily," said Sam1, rubbing at his temple.

"You were pretty indecisive out there. You showed a distinctive lack of poise," I said.

Dave Reid3 started to mumble, and then said, "What's going on? Take this thing off me."

I pulled the mask off. I handed Dave Reid a bottle of water, realized his hands were tied and then offered to hold it up to his lips. He declined. I offered to put a chip in his mouth. This he also declined.

"You guys are dead! Are you from St. Augustine's?" he asked.

Indicative of how central L-S-C's athletics were to its young psyches, Dave Reid found it conceivable that a rival high school sports team might violently kidnap him.

"It is me," I said, removing my mask, "Sam McQuiggan, but from the future!"

Sam1, not to be upstaged, also removed his mask and said, "And me, also Sam McQuiggan, from even farther in the future."

"Whoa," said Dave Reid.

"We apologize for having kidnapped you," said Sam1.

Dave Reid was in a more than a figurative bind. The situation called for incredulity. But our faces and voices told the story.

"What was the nickname we gave the girl who lived behind us when we were kids?" he asked.

"Shit factory," Sam1 and I said in unison. The girl had soiled her pants once in our presence; that was the etymology of the name.

"This is messed up. Am I hallucinating?" Dave Reid3 asked.

"Nope," said Sam1.

"What do you want with me?"

"That's where it gets complicated," I said.

"How often do you see Sam McQuiggan these days? The guy you'd know as the real Sam McQuiggan, the one who is eighteen?" asked Sam1.

"Um...."

"Let me help you with the monikers here," I said, "Call him Sam1, me Sam2, and the Sam you know is Sam3."

"Okay. But shouldn't he be Sam1, because he was here first?" asked Dave 'Reeder' Reid3.

"You'd think so but then that is not the case because..."

Sam1 cut me off. "When did you last see him? Sam3?"

"I don't know. A few months ago."

"How do you think that makes him feel?" asked Sam1.

"Makes him feel?" asked teen-aged Dave3.

"Yes."

"Fine, I guess. I don't know. Why should he feel anything?"

"Why should he feel anything," Sam1 intoned, and then whistled.

"Because of the sleepovers. Because of the jokes you fucking asshole," I more or less screamed.

"And none of your friends are even real friends!" added Sam1 in what would within the fairness of context be considered a half-scream.

"I have plenty of friends," said Dave Reid3.

"You have buddies. Buddies. Friendships of utility! Friendships of pleasure!" I said.

"Don't tell me who my friends are you old psycho," said Dave.

"Let's not start throwing insults around," Sam1 said, "We're here because...well, this is awkward. We're here because you abandoned us. Not you, but Dave1, and in Sam2's case, Dave2. You abandoned us and we never got over it. And we just keep getting worse and worse."

"What even exactly is this faggotry?" asked Dave3.

"Do not make this about our heterosexuality. This is not a gay thing," I said.

"I never got over you," Dave mimicked in a whiny voice, "Not gay though."

"Look," said Sam1, "It's a Saturday night. Do you know what Sam3 is doing?"

"How should I know?"

"He's probably hanging out with a bunch of people he hates," I said.

"How is this my problem?"

"It is a question of basic empathy. You grew up with him," said Sam1.

"No, alright. No. At some point my responsibility ended. He has decent friends, I'm sure. Sorry if my old neighbour's happiness isn't my number one priority. He's an eighteen-year-old dude."

I ate a handful of chips.

Sam2 ate a handful of chips.

We chewed on chips for a few seconds and ruminated until the exact same second when Sam1 and I both started shouting sentences like angry toddlers.

"The friends he has all suck!" I said.

While Sam1 said, "You couldn't have invited Sam3 to the post-basketball game festivities?"

"I could have, but I didn't."

"Why?" I asked.

"Because he's weird alright. He's not like the other guys and he says weird stuff and it's embarrassing for me. It's not my fault he wants to spend all his time reading dictionaries or whatever he does, acting like he's better than everybody."

More chips consumed.

"So that's how it is? Guy you were practically raised with doesn't say the same mindless shit about NHL hockey so it's easier to just throw him overboard," said Sam1.

Sam1 and I were both so angry that we decided to step out of the van for air.

"This is going nowhere fast," I said. "And he's right you know. We weren't just weird. We were imperious jerks. Needy imperious jerks. What could be worse?"

"We should just kill him," said Sam1.

We didn't kill him. I told Dave we'd be leaving him in the van overnight, and if he didn't drink water then he could conceivably die of dehydration. He took a couple swallows.

We returned to the apartment and found it empty. I picked up the cordless, hit #67 again, called Dave's step-mom and said, "Hi there, Sam is sleeping over tonight. He's just in the shower now but he wanted me to let you know."

"Thanks Sam. We noticed the car in the driveway and wondered what was going on."

I don't know why I called her. I guess it was as simple as not wanting his parents to worry. I had no idea the amount of torment it would lead to for poor Sam3. If all the worldlines of the multiverse are ever reconciled in some great beyond and Sam3 goes on to have access to this manuscript along with I guess all of the world's recorded information, then know this: Fuck, I sure am sorry man.

16

We both slept fitfully. Our sleeping bags did little to cushion bones from the hard floor. I dreamt of jail, and of Dave Reid3 imprisoned in our van. At one point I considered checking on him, but Sam1 didn't want to increase our roommates' suspicion.

The scent of microwaved Pop-Tarts woke me. We hadn't bought any breakfast foods, so I asked Blinky for a Pop-Tart. He offered to sell me one for a dollar. I invested in half the box at the cost of one twoonie, which is what Canadians call a two-dollar coin. More generous with weed than breakfast confections, Blinky invited Sam1 and me to join in the communal wake and bake. Sam1 was eager for it. Though I've never been a big weed smoker, the effects of weed having contributed to my most embarrassing drunken atrocities, the phrase, "Any port in a storm," came to mind.

Stank-Bag Sal, the roommate who would not just be implicated in Blinky's head-slicing but convicted as the accomplice who procured the cleaver, asked what our deal was. Sam1 handled the query with admirable concision.

"Just passing through to Thunder Bay. Going to get a job in forestry eh."

"Why'd you stop here?" asked Sal.

"Going to stop in Timmins too," said Sam1, and that seemed to settle the matter.

"You guys should come with us to the hockey game to-day," said Big Rog, the third of the Boar Street housemates.

"We're going to get baked and go to the Cougars game," Blinky said.

Getting baked in every sacrosanct L-S-C setting was a big deal to them. It was their way of subverting L-S-C's hockey-playing, line-towing façade of community and fellowship. It might be worth nothing that Blinky had been hated and feared in my time, though he'd posed no tangible threat outside of presenting a counter-cultural model that others might adopt. It's further worth noting that he did seem to attract the prettiest of the wayward or otherwise would-be-wayward girls.

"Maybe," said Sam1.

An hour spent in our room revealed what precious little we had to occupy our time. Nor did we yet have a plan for Reeder, prompting a heated discussion about our total lack of planning.

"We might as well go," I said after a silence of almost fifteen minutes. A silence spent doing absolutely nothing by the way. No phones to check. No TV to be watched. Just two hostile doppelgangers staring at dirty yellow walls.

"I hate hockey. You must hate hockey," said Sam1.

"Any sensible non-hockey player from L-S-C hates hockey," I said, "But here we have a chance to view the culture that spurned us. Get a sense of whether it was really so bad or if we're just angry and sick over nothing. Also, they have those one dollar hot dogs."

"That's true," Sam1 said, "But what if someone notices our condition?"

"As look-a-likes, if we want our presence to go unquestioned, it can't hurt to be among the dregs of L-S-C society."

We all piled in the red Nissan. The hockey game was like all awful hockey games. Though I realize affecting the necessary maneuvers of the sport must be difficult on skates, the in-corner grinding and spastic fluttering of the puck always appeared clumsy and aesthetically displeasing to me. I will concede that my views on hockey were warped by its disproportionate value in the L-S-C social economy and the associated effects on my teenage romantic prospects. Don't picture me as some bitter and ill co-ordinated non-athlete however. I excelled on a near provincial level at the fine sport of badminton.

Halfway through the second period the beautiful kids walked in. Those youth in the arena that could notice without judgment did so. Those adult men for whom it was inappropriate to notice also noticed but then pretended they hadn't.

There was Sherilyn. If she'd glowed at Good Feels, I had forgotten the megawatt power her skin had shone with in high school. She was followed by Jen Parisenti and Megan Goodchild, both busty, if not particularly kind. Walking in after them were little Nicole3 and Sam3.

"Hey now," said Sam1.

They sat five rows in front of us. In a panic we walked to the top of the arena and made a beeline for the concessions. We each got a bag of popcorn and two hot dogs. We crept back to our seats and hunched behind our roommates.

I heard the confectioner's sugar laugh owned by Nicole. I saw Nicole lean her head on Sam3's shoulder.

"This is it. This is exactly what was so unfair," Sam1 said in a soft voice.

"Think about what's going through his mind, what that's doing to him, the hopes being fostered this damn second," I added.

Sam1 clicked his tongue.

She had leaned into me before. I assumed Nicole1 had leaned into Sam1. But this Nicole continued to lean on Sam3. This Nicole wasn't going anywhere.

"Are they holding hands?" asked Sam1.

"They better not be. I sure hope not. I sure hope they are not holding hands," I said.

"What are you guys talking about?" asked Blinky.

"Hockey," I said.

When the period ended the girls and Sam1 walked towards the concession stand. We saw it all go down. Nicole stopped for a moment and tucked her bright blond hair behind her ears. Sam3 put his hands on her waist. Her lower lip was suppressed beneath her centrals. She gave him a mischievous look. A look that had always killed me. Sam3 pushed her against the Plexiglas and kissed her.

"Oh fuck right off," said Sam1.

We'd come back to help Sam3, but evidently Sam3 didn't need any help from us. I pictured Dave Reid3, confined to a van, abutting a temporal displacement unit. We weren't doing any good here. If anything we were going to blow it for Sam3.

"We have to go free Dave Reid3," I said.

"He'll go to the police."

"Screw it," I said, "No one will believe him, and right after we free him we take off for 2004 eh?"

We figured it easier to wait for the game's conclusion than to strand our roomies. We lived to regret the decision because it meant watching Sam3 enjoy a tenderness from Nicole3 that we'd always needed and not got. I rationalized that Sam3 would never know what it was like to suffer. Sam3 got what he needed when he needed it. To paraphrase Dr. Jessica, this very lack blessed Sam1 and me with the unenviable but profoundly-alive condition of what the analytic rumination hypothesis describes quite beautifully as 'depressive realism,' the concept that some depression is not neurologically-based but owing rather to too accurate a perception of the world's sorrow.

At the end of the game we stalled to give Nicole3 and Sam3 time to leave without seeing us. When Blinky and the boys returned to their bong we rushed to the van to make things right with Dave Reid3. But there would be no making things right with Reeder3. Dave Reid3 was dead. We had not accounted for the -21 temperature leading to that wintertime bane of all northern Ontarians: the runny nose. We had not banked on the snot congealing and leading to a stuffed nose. We had not considered that a stuffed nose in conjunction with a taped mouth would cause death by asphyxiation.

"We have killed Dave Reid3," said Sam1 after checking for a pulse.

I splashed some water from my water bottle on Dave Reid3's face.

"Your DNA is probably all up in that water," chastised Sam1. "Your DNA is Sam3's DNA. Your fingerprints are Sam3's fingerprints."

He paused.

"Your voice is Sam3's voice."

"Sam3 is going to be in bad shape," I said.

"I am taking this moment to think back on the various codes and creeds I swore to uphold," said Sam1.

"John Titor will not be enthused," I said.

Sarcasm failed to shield us from our pain. We hadn't known Dave Reid3, but he was a Dave Reid after all. We weren't from this worldline, but we weren't killers either.

"Hell," Sam1 said, and kicked at a scrap of duct tape on

the van's floor.

"Sorry Dave," I said.

"All those rides to school, all those…" said Sam1.

"Don't get into that stuff," I said. "We have to dump this body."

Body dumping sites were discussed. I suggested the St. Mike's Elementary dumpster. As a young paper boy I'd dumped my advertising circulars there because we were paid .15 cents a paper, but only .3 cents per circular, so nuts to that.

"That's right next door to Sam3's house, idiot," said Sam1.

"You got any better ideas?"

He didn't, so we covered the corpse with a bunch of garbage bags and decided a visit to Sam3 was in order.

..... ·¹ ·⁷ .....

It was heartening to see the same Honda Accord and the same Ford F150 in the driveway. It was less heartening to see the two squad cars parked across the street. Sam1 and I drove to Mac's and nervously consumed a package of nachos with one of those microwavable pouches of cheese. This was a great value at Mac's. It was the exact same nachos and cheese that cost $7.99 in 2001 dollars at the movies, really undercutting the sense of "venue-specific treat" the theatre tried to project.

When we returned to Carol Crescent the cop cars were gone. We parked three houses down and waited. After an hour Sam3 got into his mom's car and took off. We followed. He was heading to the west end, most likely to Nicole Esposito3's house. We'd both made the trip many times, and were debating leaving him be when he stopped for gas. That's when we jumped out of the car and sort of surrounded him. This was a bad introduction. Imagine seeing two older versions of yourself looking like they mean business in the Esso parking lot.

"Don't be alarmed," said Sam1.

But Sam3 was already alarmed enough to be scrambling for the driver's side door. Sam1 grabbed him by the elbow.

"Help," yelled Sam3.

I got him in a headlock and we dragged him into our car. Only then did we realize the problem of his vehicle. There were few options, so I maintained the headlock while Sam1 got in Sam3's car and parked it around the block. This was only possible because if I was a beanpole at 150, and still down to about 145 after the crash diet, Sam3, at 18, weighed no more than 125 pounds, making him easy to detain, not to mention making it that much more inconceivable he'd achieved romantic congress with a Nicole Esposito.

"Who the hell are you guys?" he asked.

I pointed to the freckle above my left eyebrow, the freckle above his left eyebrow, and the freckle above Sam1's left eyebrow.

"We are time travelers from the future young man," said Sam1, seeming rather fatherly and authoritative from the driver's seat.

"No, you're not."

What could be said?

"Yes, we are," said Sam1.

"Wait. Were you guys in that van that just showed up? Matt Gourd-Graves was in line for the Ace and he swore it literally came out of nowhere."

"That was us," I said.

"So hold on. Do you have something to do with the disappearance of Dave Reid?" he asked.

"No," I lied.

Sam1, more duplicitous than me, feigned genuine concern when he asked, "What's going on with Dave Reid?"

"He's been missing for more than a day. His step-mom said I called to say he was sleeping over. But I didn't call. I haven't hung out with Dave in months."

"And how does that make you feel?" I asked.

Sam1 crinkled his brow at me, effectively ending the discussion. Sam3 didn't seem eager to answer the question anyway.

"Look, we've established that we're you, you're us. Can we go get a beer or wings or something like civilized people," asked Sam1.

Sam3 called Nicole3 and told her he'd be an hour late. I felt slighted. You meet two future versions of yourself and that's only worth an hour of your time? Then again, had a Nicole Esposito ever been mine I wouldn't have left her waiting long either. We got wings at The Upstairs Bar and they were fantastic, just like I remembered them. There was so much batter you'd get these huge growths of batter hanging off the sides. We used to call those "cancer wings." Sam3 got a Pepsi. Sam1 and I both got triple vodka sodas in pint glasses.

"How do things go for me? From the looks of you guys, not all that well."

"Since you've given us only an hour," scolded Sam1, "We have little time to explain things like the Everett-Wheeler model, the Many Worlds Interpretation, and the concept that this worldline is not the same one we started out on. The gist is nothing that happened to us will necessarily happen to you, but most of it well may."

"We were crushed by Dave Reid's rejection of us," I blurted out, "That's the significance of this era for Sam2 and me. And for you too we imagine."

Sam1 tilted his forehead in the direction of The Upstairs Bar's fluorescent lights, exhaled through his nose, and then drank about a third of his drink in three hard gulps. He then made the 'ahh' noise.

Sam3 looked at his Pepsi, perhaps wishing it could afford him the same level of relief. In that moment I saw in him what had gotten us. More so than the rejections of Reeder and the pushing away of Bethany, it was only substances that had spoiled us, nothing more than the need to feel different.

"Screw that meathead. He wants to hang out with a bunch of mouth-breathers that's his prerogative," said Sam3.

The young man looked around, didn't see the waitress anywhere, and drank from my glass. He appeared shocked at the strength of it. It just doesn't occur to an eighteen year old to drink a triple without any kind of sugar-based mix. I was kind of steamed that he'd chosen my drink, obviously taking me for the weak sister in the operation.

"Or he doesn't want to hang out with you because you are an eighteen-year-old L-S-C resident who uses a word like *prerogative*," said Sam1.

"*Prerogative* is not an especially big or fancy word," said Sam3.

"Not so *abstruse* a word, you might say," I said, to show him that I could out-snot him any day of the week.

"Yes," said Sam1, "Yes. This is what Dave Reid cannot and will not abide."

"Why should I care what he abides? I've wheeled twice the girls he has. I have an adorable girlfriend. He could be dead for all I care."

"You don't mean that. And you haven't wheeled twice the girls," I said.

"I have."

"Name them."

He named eighteen girls. Quickly, too. He wasn't lying. The second last name was Sherilyn Drew.

"Oh no way no you didn't," said Sam1 in one breath.

He got out his 2001-era phone, and found a text from Sherilyn circa 2000 that corroborated the wheeling, which was a L-S-C-specific euphemism for sex.

"What did you do differently?" I asked, "How and why are you killing it on this worldline?"

"I don't know how to answer that," said Sam3, "How did you guys blow it so bad? I'm not saying that facetiously. I honestly want to know so I can avoid blowing it so bad my-self."

I considered dead and rotting Dave "Reeder" Reid3 and the forthcoming consequences for Sam3.

"If you date a girl named Bethany, or a sweet little girl in college—who knows maybe it will be Nicole for you—never, and I mean never, get drunk and smash a bunch of plates," said Sam1.

"That's very specific."

"Look, if you get this plate smashing urge, know that that's where it all goes astray. Look at that man's sunken dead eyes," I said, indicating Sam1.

Sam1 ordered another round.

"Another Pepsi too?" asked the waitress.

Sam1 gave her a look to convey that no one ever needs a second round of Pepsi.

"This is going to take more than an hour isn't it?" asked Sam3.

It did. We drove down the town's sad little laneways, past the McMansions in the rich part of town, through its antiquated downtown core and the newly dug construction craters for the big box stores that would soon kill the downtown core.

"I'm not sure if this is good advice or not," said Sam1, "But I always figured if I hadn't left for university, if I'd stayed here in L-S-C forever, that I'd have been much happier."

"I'd have to agree. Plus you seem to have it much better than us to begin with. What with the eighteen wheelings of St. Mark's Collegiate elites."

"Did you guys like never have sex in high school or something?"

"I prefer not to comment," said Sam1

"Very few times, I'll say," said I.

"Like five times?"

"This isn't about cocksmanship," yelled Sam1. "It is about personal satisfaction. It is about leading a healthy life not filled with regret. It is about the womb of L-S-C you must not leave."

"I'm not staying here," said Sam3 with some haughtiness, "You can't be a screenwriter and live here."

Screenwriter. I almost laughed.

"We all thought that," I said. "You're right of course. But we all thought that. Both of us left the first chance we got. And there are exactly zero fucking screenwriters sitting at this table right now."

A not-uncordial silence followed.

"What do you guys want to do?" Sam3 asked, as though we were just three buddies out cruising the town. "My parents are at the Lion's Club for a Super Bowl party until at least ten tonight. We can chill at my place."

Risk of police surveillance didn't come up, so that's

where we chilled. And there was the linoleum of my youth, and there were my mom's teddy bears, the baby pictures of me or of an identical Sam3, my tire swing in the back yard by the bent basketball hoop, the standard three bags of Tostitos in the cupboard beside the fridge. Sam1 took a deep breath and then actually got down on his hands and knees and smelled the linoleum.

"Can we try not being weird for like two seconds?" asked Sam3.

He conveyed a certain charm that had been lacking in me. I wouldn't have handled linoleum smelling so coolly. He got out a bag of Tostitos and some cheese dip and Sam1 and I enjoyed our second nacho snack of the day. Sam3 said he had half a bottle of Fireball Whiskey in his room if we wanted some. We were able to decline, perhaps not requiring the buttressment of spicy spirits while in the comfort of such familiar kitchen fixtures.

"Boy, I hope things are different for you," said Sam1, again sounding paternal, "But for us, it never got better than these days in this kitchen, even without Dave Reid or Nicole. This was it."

"It's not even that nice of a kitchen," said Sam3.

I knew I had to tell the kid about his Dave Reid. But I didn't have it in me. Not that night. We said our goodbyes and drove back to the apartment.

Blinky looked at us for a solid twenty second interval after we'd entered the household, like maybe he didn't remember who we were. In his defense, Blinky was exhaling a massive cloud of bong smoke for most of that twenty second interval.

"Whoa, for a minute there I thought you guys were like some future version of Sam McQuiggan but like double."

In the bedroom I said to Sam1, "Why not frame one of

these idiots for Dave Reid's death?'"

When everyone had fallen asleep I crept into the living room and clicked the icon for their dialup Internet connection. Blinky's Hotmail account was still logged in. I sent an incriminating missive to one of his friends, Justin Springer. This name seemed right to me. In my experience drug dealers and low-lifes were often named Justin. Stupid as Blinky and probably Justin were, I couldn't make it too overtly incriminating; Justin would likely respond after all. So I kept it just cryptic enough to bypass Blinky's powers of deduction.

"The 'Deeder' is done!" I emailed Justin Springer.

–18–

The next morning Sam1 woke with a hitherto unseen level of energy and purpose and said, "Sam2, we are dumping that body."

I nodded with an approximation of stoicism, for it was stoicism I wished to exude but revulsion over the task at hand that I felt. I then microwaved two Pop Tarts.

"Remember that line from *The Simpsons*: 'Men, put on your corpse handling gloves,'" I asked Sam1, "We may now legitimately need corpse handling gloves."

We drove to Canadian Tire and purchased rubber gloves, bleach, lye, heavy-duty garbage bags, industrial strength deodorizer, and a family-sized package of Slim-Jims that was on sale. As fate had it, the same cashier who'd rung in our baseball bat/ski mask purchase manned the register we paid at. If she remembered us she gave no indication.

The oft-described but seldom-experienced reek of death greeted us when we opened the door to the van. We'd forgotten something to cover our noses. The body's partially frozen state made it impossible to unbend the legs and stuff it in a garbage bag. Sam1 held the torso while I pulled at the legs. They barely budged. We bashed at the legs with the bat for a while and then gave up. We ended up not putting Dave Reid3 in the garbage bags so much as taping the garbage bags all around Dave Reid3.

The hope of a strategic dumping site was foregone in favour of quick disposal. We drove around until we saw a dumpster beside Mrs. Vespasian's west end location. They didn't open until 11 am and the parking lot was empty. We struggled to get the ungainly mass out of the van. Once it was finally in the dumpster it jutted up in an unfortunate way, so we dumped more garbage bags over it.

"What about the lye?" I asked.

When Sam1 ineffectually dumped a few shakes of lye over the garbage bags themselves, it became clear that he had even fewer insights into the application of lye than I did.

"That's not going to do anything," I yelled.

"I don't know," he yelled.

At that point Sam1 climbed into the dumpster and began jumping up and down on Reeder's corpse. The combined force of his weight plus gravity eventually broke through the rigor mortis and crumbled Dave Reid3's bones into a reasonable sized pile that was less likely to be discovered by Mrs. Vespasian or whatever member of the Vespasian family first visited the dumpster.

"I need a drink," I said, though it was only 10 am.

"I would like to attend a mass," said Sam1, "There's an 11:30 one at St. Mary's Cathedral."

The LCBO didn't open until noon, and I hated to be one of those guys just waiting outside the door for it to open, so I attended service with Sam1. The church was ornate as I'd remembered. It had been years since I'd been to mass. I'd also never been to a mid-week service. There was a higher level of piety. People might go on a Sunday because it was the thing to do, or to be seen, or to be with family, but weekday worshipers were there because of a crushing certainty that God was observing and judging and best of all forgiving their sins. It called to mind something John Cheever had written, "These are earnest people, mostly old, making an organized response to the mysteriousness of life." Even I, a casual agnostic, called on God for forgiveness that morning. When Sam1 lit a votive candle, ostensibly to cleanse us of us our sins, I was glad that he did.

We got cheeseburgers at Mary's Diner and then bought a sixty ounce bottle of Smirnoff at the LCBO. Though we might get caught by the police at any minute for dumping a body, and should have been taking care of business and getting ready to jump to 2004, all we did was go back to our apartment and get piss drunk.

At an early stage in our bender Sam1 decided to be proactive and set the Temporal Displacement Unit's co-ordinates for 2004. He wasn't quite ready to leave this worldline, but deemed it advisable in case a quick exit became necessary. I watched him at the controls. It was much easier than he'd made it out to be. Basically nothing more than setting a date, time, latitude and longitude. The gravitic tidal forces he'd snootily mentioned during our first departure were all completely automated. I figured I could set the coordinates in a pinch.

It doesn't take many hours of sitting around an unfurnished single room drinking warm vodka-sodas with an aged and surly double before a man gets the urge for some air. We decided on a trip to the corner Mac's Mart for ice and soda. As we stood in the parking lot something about the fresh, good air of our respective childhoods chastised us.

"We aren't here much longer," said Sam1, "And all we're doing is sitting in a room like a couple of death's door-type losers."

"What do you feel like doing?" I asked, "Entertainment options have always been limited in this shit town."

Sam1 checked his watch. It was 3:25 pm. Sam3 would be getting off school and heading home to deliver his paper route. Assuming no divergence, his parents wouldn't get home from their jobs until after 6 pm. Sam1 drove drunkenly but cautiously to Carol Court. I do not mean to downplay the seriousness of drinking and driving, but it's fairly *de rigueur* in L-S-C. I'd been doing it since I was licensed to drive. The town elders did it. The politicians and Junior-A hockey stars alike. The benchmark for "too many drinks" was generally higher in L-S-C. In Toronto you might get a dirty look after two or three drinks. In L-S-C it was closer to twenty.

When we saw Sam3 delivering his papers, Sam1 rolled down the window and hollered, "Hey paper boy, give me a paper," in a caricature of some drunken local goon. Though only one street over from our relatively posh one, our paper route had been home to a number of deadbeats. Some of those characters still owe me like eighty dollars on my world-line.

Sam3 couldn't help but smile. It was something, to see your own sense of humour, but developed and darkened over the years, and then delivered in your own voice, at you. Sam3 threw a paper through the open driver's side window.

"Hurry up. We'll be back at your place," said Sam1.

It wasn't yet necessary to lock your doors in

Lac-Sainte-Catherine because this era pre-dated the Oxy epidemic by several years, meaning Purdue had not yet deemed it financially prudent to steal the town's dignity. We helped ourselves to the well-stocked McQuiggan fridge. They had ice, for example, and clean glasses, and things like pickled eggs. The drinks tasted infinitely better with ice.

When Sam3 returned we mixed him a strong drink, but squeezed in plenty of lemon. It was a hell of a thing to do. I didn't drink my first triple until I was at least twenty-two. Start someone that early and there's nowhere to go but down. Once you get into quads you are out of mixed drink territory altogether and essentially drinking straight liquor.

We started telling bullshit stories, as was the norm in L-S-C. Sam1 boasted of athletic accomplishments that I considered dubious. I boasted of the student short story prize I'd legitimately won in 2002. Sam3 boasted of his multitude of sex partners. We looked through his yearbooks and noted minor divergences.

We recollected one traumatic memory shared by us all. A story had gotten around and gained traction around grade eleven, that we, each of us Sams, had peed in a communion chalice before the big confirmation ceremony in grade eight. Know that none of us had pissed in a communion chalice. But *Beavis and Butthead* had been popular at the time, and, I anyway—can't speak to the specific details for Sam1 and Sam3 here—said to my friend Brett Tomkin, in a pew, awaiting communion, in maybe a Beavis impression, "Let's piss in the chalice, eh-heh, eh-heh, eh-heh." Those at my elementary school of St. Matthew's knew no chalice pissing had occurred, but it got around to other elementary schools that I had indeed desanctified that gold cup of the Lord's transubstantiated blood. This rumour was somehow revived and picked up steam two years later in grade ten and was all but established fact by grade eleven. Classmates who'd attended my elementary school either misremembered the non-incident as a real incident, or maliciously refused to debunk the rumour. I'd learned of the rumour waiting for a ride at my mom's dental office one day. Kathryn Palumbo had been there for a cleaning. She'd always been excruciatingly kind, and kind of sad, like having to be so kind all the time made her sad, and she'd said, "You didn't really pee in the chalice did you?" From that point on, I had to make this terrible effort to go around telling people the Beavis and Butthead story and how it was Beavis homage and not actual urinary blasphemy I'd committed. Both Beavis and Butthead were by that time somewhat passé, and having to do the eh-he, eh-he, eh-he laugh to illustrate my story just seemed vulgar, but it was better than having people think I relieved myself in a chalice, because at least among the upper echelons of St. Mark's Collegiate society we were a very conservative group of teenagers.

We played two games of Madden 2001 on Sam3's PS1. He asked about the advancements to come in the Madden franchise, which I tried my best to describe, but he looked deflated by my laboured descriptions of the "truck stick" and "lead tackle controls" and so forth. He'd figured you'd be tackling and throwing passes with your physical body in some ultra-real simulation by 2016. To this end we told him about the Nintendo Wii, and how the Wii kind of sucked and would end up being a passing fad, and that he shouldn't be one of the early adopters.

"Let's order some wings," said Sam1, starting to sound quite drunk.

"Can't," slurred Sam3, without question drunk as fury, "Parents will be home soon."

We placed a pickup order for wings and spuds at Fred's Fried Chicken and drove to pick it up. Sam1 was starting to veer slightly, but never quite left the confines of his lane. We took our takeout to Bellamy Field where it filled the car with the odour of its holy grease. The concept that scent is the closest sense linked to memory was not lost on Sam1, who spent at least thirty seconds inhaling from the bag.

"Remember ordering these with Reeder in grade ten and watching wrestling?" he asked me.

"Speaking of Reeder," said Sam3, "He's still missing. It's getting pretty scary. Two days now. Not a word. There was an announcement at school today."

Sam1 looked like he was going to say something. Instead he opened the bucket of spuds. Two great things about Fred's Fried Chicken: 1) all their food came in buckets, which you often saw on television but rarely in real life, and 2) the dipping sauce that came with the spuds was simple: sour cream and ranch dressing, but it was world class.

Sam1 let out a low and rather off-putting moan when he bit into his first dunked spud, quelling any further discussion of Dave Reid3's disappearance and death. After our meal we once again found ourselves without ice. We drank a few warm drinks but the bloom was leaving the rose. Suddenly we were just two old drunks ruining the life of a fresh-faced kid and digesting greasy chicken. Is this what we'd come back for? Fred's Fried Chicken?

Sam3 vomited out the rear door. He rinsed his mouth with his drink and seemed revived. I took a moment to marvel at the resiliency of youth.

"I know what we have to do. Nicole has to meet you guys," Sam3 said.

Sam1 and I both drank from our plastic cups.

"I'm serious, I'm serious you guys," said Sam1 in one drunken rush of words. "When else is she going to get a chance to meet the future me?"

His argument was sound. Sam1 and I decided to talk it over outside the car.

"You really want to see her?"

"I want to see what's different about her. If she's kinder than our Nicoles, and maybe that's why Sam3 got her, or if she's the same, and he's just superior to us," said Sam1.

L-S-C living had a way of sweeping you up in the circumstances of the night. You might be driving around with some pals, and then it's decided the pals want to visit the home of your worst enemy, or a girl you'd impregnated who'd recently aborted your prospective offspring. You wanted off the ride, but you couldn't exactly jump out of the car and onto the hard King Street pavement.

We drove to her house and waited a block away. Fifteen minutes later Sam3 was running back to the car with the girl on one arm and chunks of firewood in the other. She got in the backseat with him and gasped.

"I didn't believe you, but wow," she said.

I was also in a state of disbelief. It was her. With those sing-song vowels and pink crescent lips.

"Hi Nicole," I said.

She did a double take.

"And the same voice," she said.

Sam3 pointed out the trifecta of matching freckles.

Sam1 had been hitting the bottle hard in preparation for this reunion and slurred significantly when he asked Sam3, "Where to now?"

I wasn't sure how Sam3 had taken over leadership responsibilities for the night. Maybe because he was younger, and drunker, and thus the better reveller, or maybe because he had the swing to land Nicole and we didn't.

"Ojibway Provincial Park," he said, "For a bonfire."

That park was an hour's drive away, but it was a mild night, and Sam3 did have the wood. We stopped for a newspaper and some lighter fluid. The front page told of Dave Reid's disappearance, so I put it under the passenger seat to avoid dampening the mood.

It did not take many sips from Sam3's glass to get Nicole roaring drunk, which helped distract from any pertinent time travel-related questions that should have been on her mind. Instead she chirped bird-like noises about Sherilyn's recent birthday party, some boots she wished to buy in Toronto, and how much she loved Sam3. I was happy to listen. I had always liked listening to her little voice.

It's not hard to get a fire going when you have lighter fluid, and the leftover chicken made for an excellent snack to absorb the booze. We were glad we'd gotten one-hundred-and-twenty wings, which had seemed excessive when Sam1 placed the order.

The park was deserted at this time of year, allowing us to pull right up to the fire pit and blare The Otter. When Tom Petty's *Runnin' Down a Dream* came on I asked Nicole to dance. Sam3 seemed fine with this. It wasn't really a slow song, but I slow danced with her anyway.

"I'm really glad you're with Sam3. He deserves you."

"Aww," she said, "Thank you."

I pulled her a little closer to me.

"You never got with me on my worldline."

"What's a worldline?"

"I lived this same life but without you."

"That's so sad," she said, and sounded like she meant it.

Sam3 was showing Sam1 some kind of wrestling maneuver that involved lifting Sam1 over his head. Both of them nearly fell in the fire.

"Settle down over there boys," I hollered.

I asked Nicole if she wanted to go for a walk. She agreed.

"You two better not be going to wheel," cackled Sam3. He then laughed the laugh of a much older and more horrible drunk. I could hear myself in him. Surely I'd sounded like that on too many nights in my early twenties, and on the bad night.

I took Nicole's hand in mine and led her over some logs and branches and things. I stopped Nicole and kissed her on the mouth.

"I shouldn't," she said, "But you look so much like him. Only more manly."

"Because I'm thirty-one years old," I said.

"Oh," she said.

She kissed me. The whole ordeal, even the death of Dave 'Reeder' Reid3, seemed more or less worth it to me then.

The bottle was near empty so we decided to drive back. Sam1 tripped over a log and landed face first on the way to the car. It was decided I should drive. I kept sneaking glances at Nicole in the rear view mirror. She slept like a small animal in Sam3's arms. I'd had but a small taste of Sam3's existence. But I knew the kid had it good. Though it meant an extra fifty minutes of driving we dropped Nicole off first because that was the gentlemanly thing to do.

"I love you guys," said Sam3 near his home, "I really do."

"We love you too," I said.

19

We woke the next morning on our sleeping bags, which was the best possible outcome. I had an extremely dry mouth and reached for a glass of water situated between Sam1 and myself.

"That's my water," he said.

"We share the same DNA I think we can share a glass of water."

That old hangover restlessness prevented me from falling back asleep. It's a cruel condition. You're tired as hell, but so jittery you just have to get up and commence with the day's ragged ordeal. Sam1 had a favourite biblical quote, from the Book of Joel, "Awake, ye drunkards and weep; and howl, all ye drinkers of wine."

"I kissed her," I said, "It was incredible."

"You think I don't know that? You wouldn't shut up about it last night."

"My bad," I said. "You could have kissed her too, probably."

"I am over fifty years old. There are certain limits of propriety to which I subscribe," said Sam1.

I reached for another sip of water.

"Get your own goddamn water," Sam1 screamed.

He reached for the water and it spilled all over us both. He grabbed me by the collar of my t-shirt and slammed me against the wall. I got hold of his shirt and pushed him as hard as I could. We both fell through the door and onto the living room floor. Sam1 got me in a headlock and started punching the top of my head. I had my face buried in the ground, so all he could hit was skull. It was probably hurting his hand more than it did my head.

Our new roommates weren't making any sudden moves to break up the fight. In classic L-S-C fashion they were cheering on the fight, in fact chanting the words, "Fight! Fight! Fight!" as was pretty much the only known response to a fight in L-S-C.

Sam1 decided he was getting nowhere punching my skull and began punching me in the neck. This proved unsustainable so I used all of my strength to lift him off the ground. I couldn't hold him for long and we both fell in the direction of the boys, knocking the large glass bong off the table. We then wrestled in a puddle of stale bongwater until Sam1 found himself in the full mount position on top of me. He pulled back his fist, all ready to break my face, and then I guess the better angels of his nature won out.

"Aww man," said Blinky. Whether it was the fight's cessation or the spilled bong-water upsetting him was not clear.

The boys sentenced us to clean up the spill. There wasn't much to be done though, given the household's dearth of cleaning supplies. We ended up soaking up as much of the bong water as we could with Kleenex, but most of it had already sunk into the hardwood floor. We looked at Big Rog for approval. There was an unspoken consensus that the floor was just going to smell like stale bong water going forward and there was nothing to be done about it. We went back to our room and brooded.

"Sorry man," I said after a while.

"I was just sore because I wanted to kiss her too," said Sam1.

"Maybe we could see them again tonight," I said.

"We can't start a new life here, you idiot," said Sam1, but not without affection.

We heard a business-intending knock on the unit's door. Blinky looked through the peephole and then scrambled to hide the weed and related paraphernalia.

"Police! We'd like to ask you a few questions. Are the tenants in the unit?"

Big Rog scrambled for some Febreeze, a recent entry into the market in 2001 and still considered something of a miracle product.

"Sirs, we have your landlord with us, and she is willing to let us in if you aren't."

Sam1 was already opening the window. We'd noted a fire escape when we first moved in. It was one of those old-time ones you had to detach each separate component of and let each component drop down. We had no idea how to separate the components, and looked at each other in pure panic. Finally through blind groping the first component cascaded down. It made a terrible racket, drawing the cops to our bedroom window. It was only a one story drop so after an exchanged glance we let ourselves fall. I landed pretty smoothly. Sam1 landed with too much weight on his left leg and then limped towards the van. I was wearing only my jeans and a t-shirt. It was fortunate that Sam1 still had the keys to the van on him. It was less fortunate that I had to run across frozen concrete in bare feet. The cops weren't willing to risk the drop, so we had a minute before they made it out of the building to lock ourselves in the van.

"Good thing we set it in advance," I said as the TDU powered up. "Where did you set it for?"

"The baseball field in the middle of High Park," Sam1 said.

Sam1 sat down in the TDU. I rubbed at my feet, burning from the cold.

One of the cops banged on the van's window. Much cliched language really does come into play in real-world discourse, and here the phrase, "Come out with your hands up," was issued.

The L-S-C City Police thought they had time on their side, and that they could wait us out. They thought the investigation was over. Just by showing up chez Blinky/Big Rog they had cracked the case. Another heroic bust and soon we the panicked and overmatched criminals would rot in Penetanguishene for the murder of Dave Reid. We knew that wasn't so, and that time was on our side, for we were the masters of time! As the machine roared to life I wondered if the cops closest to the van would be exposed to life-shortening radiation. Another atrocity perpetrated in our quest to right the wrongs that had spoiled our stupid souls. Oh well.

It wasn't long into our journey before we realized we were heinously dehydrated and wouldn't have any water to drink for three hours. I licked at my lips.

"I'm so tired," said Sam1.

"Have a nap or something."

"I can't sleep with you on top of me," said Sam1.

"I am never drinking again," I said.

"A statement that rings familiar."

"We didn't even say hello to mom and dad," I said.

"They wouldn't have wanted that," said Sam1, "I'm only two years younger than dad on that worldline. How weird would that be?"

"We regained our water weight," I said, hoping to change the subject, and also hoping maybe we would burn up that instant and be freed from our thirst and sore left sides. "We're overweight."

"Oh yeah," said Sam1. "I guess the weight protocols err

on the side of caution."

"All that cabbage for nothing," I said.

We landed where and when we wanted. July 21, 2004. Two weeks before Smash Day. I stepped out of the machine and stretched my legs. The first thing I noticed was an overwhelming sulphuric reek. I started to gag but then managed to hold onto what little was in my stomach.

"Did you shit your pants?" inquired Sam1.

"I did not shit my pants. The smell seems to be atmospheric."

"Oh man, I hope there wasn't nuclear war or something on this worldline," he said.

Sam1 checked the divergence. His initial divergence had been 1.4%. On Sam3's worldline it had been 2.8%. Now we were up to 5.6%.

"This could be trouble," he said.

"Where can I buy pants at four in the morning?" I asked.

"Not sure," said Sam1, "At least its summer."

"Care to offer me your pants?"

"I do not."

Driving out of the park we noticed a sleeping homeless man.

"Say, why don't we divest him of his pants?" I asked.

We crept up to him like a couple of vaudevillian creep caricatures. Sam1 reached forward and unclasped the man's belt. The man stirred. Sam1 gave it a minute and went back at it. He started jerking at the pants and it became clear the man would not wake. I also needed his boots. When it was all said and done I had a pair of crusty, piss-stinking pants to my name and a pair of boots that were communicating fungal infections unknowable. Fortunately the man had my approximate waist line and had notched a hole in his belt that was just about right.

Once more we found ourselves without a plan. At least it was easier to rent a flophouse room in Toronto than it was in L-S-C. After eating $32 worth of McDonalds, we plopped down $86 and had a room for two weeks. When sleep wouldn't come we decided to drive by the house where we'd shared the upstairs apartment with Bethany. There was no home to be seen. The whole block was an abandoned Future Shop, which may seem like a cute name under the circumstances, but it was only a franchise electronics store in Canada.

"I bet we can find them at Endocrine," said Sam1.

"I can't wear these pants to Endocrine. They smell," I said.

I'd first been brought to Endocrine by my roommates during our second year of university. We'd all lived in residence together in first year, and assumed our second year lodgings would be some kind of bachelor paradise. Being unfamiliar with the vagaries of the market we ended up in a unit that was nothing but one long hallway with four bedrooms jutting off at unexpected angles. Clearly our opportunistic landlord was in the business of jamming as many bedrooms as he could into every possible inch of living space. The apartment's layout was far from our biggest problem. None of us had ever lived alone, and issues like dish washing, shower scrubbing and toilet paper purchasing were constant sources of strife and discord.

On a Friday night in October of 2003 my first-ever E kicked in when the roomies and I were halfway to Endocrine.

All our petty gripes against one another ceased to matter. The guys again seemed like the bros they'd been in first year—bros to replace my bygone bros of yesteryear.

Endocrine itself was an entrée into a newer, better life in Toronto. It wasn't filled with the drunken youths I was accustomed to seeing at bars. There was a bit of everything: lawyers in Versace dress shirts, babes wearing nothing above the waste but paint, contemptible people-pleasers offering light shows.

The beat hit me as beats no doubt hit all first-time ecstasy users, and within minutes I had abandoned my group to forge new friendships among the Endocrine crowd. At one point I found myself behind the DJ booth with the DJ's inner circle. At another point two girls unbuttoned my dress shirt and kissed me in a booth for an hour. I would have enjoyed their company longer, but as our mouths grew dry, water beckoned, and at the bar I struck up a conversation with some middle-aged orthodontist that seemed so deep and meaningful that I never reconnected with those two lovely young women. It's comical: the embarrassment of riches the young can plow through in even one night, never conceiving how eager and near does the social, sexual, and psychic thief of older age lurk.

It wasn't long before I wanted to go to Endocrine every night, but pills, cover charges, and the $5 - $10 tips I was inclined to give bartenders for a glass of water were costing too much. So I started selling pills at the club. It was low risk. The bartenders and bouncers all turned a blind eye.

In March of that year I went to an after-party on UofT campus where I met Bethany. I stayed in her room for two straight days and nights, first taking endless E, and then coming down with her while she made us Ramen noodles in the communal kitchen. Her straight-laced friends were unimpressed with my presence there, describing me using the catch-all phrase "sketched out" with some regularity, and eventually demanding I leave. Bethany had always been something of a pushover, but I convinced her to take a stand for me then, and she did. A few weeks later I'd entered her apartment and heard a loud argument coming from Bethany's bedroom.

"He's creepy," said one of the friends.

"You don't see the good side of him," Bethany had said, "You don't see how sweet he can be."

It was true. I had been capable of a tenderness that none of Bethany's crow-like roommates would experience in their lives. But they'd been correct in their "creepy" assessment for that very reason. The higher the potential for good in a person the more likely he'll be compromised by agents of the archfiend.

At the front entrance the bouncer gave my hobo pants and work boots a discriminating look, but it was 5:30 am, and not many new patrons were coming in at the time. Clubs like Endocrine survive on cover charges rather than alcohol sales, so instead of closing at 3 am they closed at 8 am. Once inside, the music hit me. Sam1 closed his eyes. Sound being right behind scent in terms of senses linked to memory.

"Let's get some E," he said.

I liked the sound of that. By 2016 no one said E anymore. They said Molly. It would always be E to me. I saw a familiar-looking drug dealer in a Leafs Jersey. After some haggling I handed him a twenty and he handed me two tablets with green crosses on them.

"Have you seen Sam McQuiggan?" I asked.

By this point in my own timeline I would have been known by name to certain parties, to Leafs Jersey anyway, a competitor. I never did learn his name though, always having signified him with the words *Leafs Jersey*.

"This is weird. But I actually thought you were Sam McQuiggan. Too many pills," he said, and laughed. "He was here earlier. I think he left for The Womb."

The Womb was the irreputable older sibling to Endocrine. It didn't open until 8 am, and caught the runoff from rave-oriented clubs like Endocrine and Guvernment, all-night gay clubs, Russian and Vietnamese gangster meetings, you name it.

We swallowed our pills and mingled. I had a lovely conversation with some Ryerson teens. Sam1 was also in a pretty darn serious heart-to-heart with some youthful people. He was shouting clichés about living for the moment, and not letting youth pass them by. The youths were nodding along, locked into furious eye contact with Sam1 like he was a prophet. As luck had it his new best pals were also on their way to The Womb.

Outside, one of the girls in our party said, "Oh my God the air is so fresh!" I could recall this feeling upon leaving the club. Your senses are heightened to the max, but you've been in a sweaty basement for six hours, so that first breath of fresh air causes your lungs to tingle. Except this air was how I imagine Andre the Giant's farts smelled after he'd consumed 120-odd beers. At least her comment confirmed for me there hadn't been some Airborne Toxic Event we had to worry about lacking immunity to. This was simply how this worldline smelled. The sulphuric allusion to hell was not lost on me however.

During the twenty-minute walk Sam1 kept squeezing one guy's shoulder to make some point about the glory of youth. Maybe the E hit him harder because his organs were twenty years more shot than mine.

Inside The Womb we struck it lucky again. One member of our party ran up to a scrawny young guy and gave him a prolonged hug. There he was, Sam4, with a big smile on his face seldom smiled by any undrugged Sam McQuiggan. Soon we were seated at a large booth with our target. It was dark, and we kept our heads down.

I took a moment to watch Sam4 holding court, telling stories he had no right to tell, as though he were Scarface himself and not some punk who'd sold about $1000 worth of ecstasy in his entire life. Everyone laughed and nodded. Bethany4 came and sat down on Sam4's lap. I almost didn't want a good look at her, not while on ecstasy and full of love for the human condition. It would be hard not to reach over and press my face against hers, and what would Sam4 think of that?

Sam4 bragged of hosting an after party. There wasn't a lot of RSVPing or guest listing going on. If we followed them we'd be in. We stuck to the back of the group. I initiated conversation with a couple of forty-ish gay men. Sam1 continued talking to teens. When things inevitably soured with the teens Sam1 joined my conversation, but I gave him a jerky head nod to suggest, "We shouldn't be seen side-by-side, fool."

After a few blocks I realized Sam4 was leading the gang to the very apartment I'd shared with those roommates in second year. On my worldline Bethany2 had freed me from it and I'd moved in with her during the summer. In theirs they must have kept that shitty little room and lived in it together. I was relieved to see none of the alternate versions of my old roommates were there. Things had not ended well with those jerks.

Bethany4 and Sam4 led about half the contingent into their bedroom, probably to snort ketamine. Sam1 went in the bathroom, came out, and whispered to me, "There's some concealer in there, go put it over your eye freckle. And slick back your hair or something. You have the exact same hair-do as Sam4."

No hairstyle innovations in over a decade, sad really.

The E started to wear off and the usual depression set in. I looked at the goofy kids on the bacterially-enriched couch and wondered the usual question of, "What am I doing here?" In this case it was given extra weight by the fact that I was an extradimensional wayfarer.

Sam1 invited me outside and asked, "Did you see the note on Ryan's door? It's an ad for a subletter. You're going to take down the number and sublet that room off Ryan."

We left without saying goodbye to our hosts. We didn't need to see them in that room, spaced out on K, young and beautiful as we'd never be again. We tossed and turned in our depressing little rented flop. We didn't have weed, music, 5htp or any of the other tried and true come-down aids, leaving us no palliative but time itself, ironic since the one thing that could be depended on to ease all substance-related sorrows was the thing we were fucking with at every turn. After getting some sleep we ate another $36 worth of McDonalds.

"Gross," said Sam1, after he'd finished his double quarter pounder meal, six McNuggets, and apple pie.

"We should have eaten something nutritious," I said.

We looked at the novelty stores along Spadina. Wigs were considered and tried on. A wig would do more harm than good, it became apparent, leading us to the Lillian H. Smith library to consult the Internet. The best advice for changing a man's appearance was a drastic haircut, growing or shaving a full beard, and wearing sun-glasses. We had my head shaved for only $5 at a barbershop in Chinatown. I vowed not to shave, though I'd never grown a full beard and knew it would be like a Keanu Reeves beard at best.

"Sam2, you are going to be the type of individual who wears sunglasses at all times."

"Ah, that most suspect of individuals," I said.

"Sam2, that attitude is not going to fly with the near-teens you will be cavorting with and observing. You need to buckle down, monitor Sam4, and if the plate smashing night starts to run a familiar course, you do whatever it takes to prevent it."

"Like what?"

"You distract him. You keep him in a good mood. You break his bottle of Scotch by accident. You subdue him physically if it comes down to it," said Sam2.

"Fine, although I am a little miffed at taking on the lion's share of the responsibility here."

"And you'll need to talk differently."

I practised higher voices, more effeminate voices, but the only one that sounded realistic was a deeper voice. Regrettable, since my voice was in the James Earle Jones-range to begin with.

I called Ryan and said we'd meet to provide him with three months' rent that afternoon. Ryan didn't balk when his potential tenant was an older dude with a freshly shaved head baring a strong resemblance to the fictional murderous Taxi Driver Travis Bickle. Here's why I called my old roommates jerks earlier. Ryan was willing to let any terrifying creep move in with his one-time friend, the unworldly Sam4.

Parking by the rooming house was costing a fortune, and there was a risk someone might break into the van and damage the TDU. We agreed that the best option was for Sam1 to drive the van out to Pearson airport and pay for a month of long-term parking. Sam1 and I shared a meal of Quizno's at the rooming house and then parted ways.

I experienced separation anxiety after having spent the last month in Sam1's constant company. I also felt a pleasant sense of freedom, like I was free of some cruelly-predictive mirror that had been affixed to me.

..... 21 .....

I steeled myself at the back entrance to 15 McCaul Street. Bethany4 or Sam4 might answer the door, and there I'd be standing like The Terminator in shades I could not remove.

The door was answered by a fifty-year-old man. It turned out Ryan wasn't the first to rent his room to an aged deviant. This guy's name was Marty, and he was the only one home at the time. After requisite introductions Marty launched into a long spiel detailing his recently-kicked addiction to meth, his necessary departure from San Bernardino, California, and his quest to find work as a mill and lathe man in Toronto. Marty lit a cigarette and went into a thirty-minute diatribe about yet another sub-letter, Kathleen, whom Marty believed had stolen a new credit card he'd been mailed.

Finally he came around to the people I was interested in, "A couple young kids. The original tenants. They're alright. The guy sells E. You do E?" Marty didn't give me a chance to answer. "I've been buying E off the kid and doing half an E. I probably shouldn't because of the amphetamine problem, but then there's probably not much speed in E anyway. Right?"

Who was I to confirm or deny this hope of Marty's?

I left for my room and laid down my sleeping bag and collection of shirts and pants from Giant Tiger. I'd existed for ten mostly-awful years to put this second-year hellhole behind me, and there I was stuck back in it.

Marty announced that he was going to look for work. I wondered why he didn't just send out some emails, but I guess in 2004 a man still went door to door, or at least a man like Marty did. Marty confided in me that he had taken half an E to fuel his quest. I'd have been altogether fine not knowing this. I feared Marty was grooming me as a potential confidant or ally.

I remembered that while each bedroom had a lock, the locks could easily be picked with a paring knife. I'm no Mac-Gyver, as these pages have illustrated; this was as simple as sticking the knife's tip in the keyhole and twisting to the right. I picked the door that had once been mine.

Bethany4 had packed up all of Sam4's dirty clothes and put them in clear plastic Ikea shelves. Things like Ikea shelves wouldn't have entered Sam4's life without Bethany4's influence. I saw a small chalk board with the words, "I love you," written on it in a feminine script. I saw a big pile of pills and three vials of K. I took a bump of K and became woozy. I lay down on the bed. Bethany's lotions and other scented products perfumed the once-stinking space. I put my face in a pillow and inhaled. Then I heard someone on the front porch and scrambled to get out of Sam4 and Bethany4's room so as not to be seen as some perverted violator of personal space on day one of my stakeout.

Sam4 and Bethany4 entered the apartment. I stood glassy-eyed in the middle of the hall, directly across from their bedroom—at worst, a stranger; at best, or perhaps worse yet, some random dude from a recent after party.

"I'm Stephen," I said, the ketamine making Sam4 appear like something of a spiral. "You can call me Steve."

No one said anything. It dawned on me that I had not relayed the pertinent information.

"I'm renting Ryan's room."

"Glad to have you man!" said Sam4. He was holding a large LCBO bag and appeared half drunk.

I shook his hand. I shook Bethany4's hand. Bethany4 didn't so much spiral as swirl. Even anti-clockwise she projected an interior winsomeness that no Facebook photo could ever convey.

"Let's have a drink," said Sam4.

I was present in this time and place to discourage this very vice, yet I knew a drink would steady me. Sam4 poured two double scotches over ice while Bethany4 unpacked groceries. I had little doubt who'd paid for the spinach and tomatoes and bottles of Diana Sauce. Sam4 would have claimed he didn't need groceries, that he was content to live on Ramen and McDonalds, but the Sam2 I'd been had had no problem consuming the elaborate meals paid for on Bethany2's credit card.

Sam4 went into his bedroom and started blaring Tom Waits. "Have you ever heard of this guy man? Tom Waits? He's amazing."

Everyone has heard of Tom Waits, thirty-one-year-old's know, but at some point in every young Tom Waits fan's heart they consider the gravel-voiced troubadour some secret diamond. I needed to make an ally of Sam4 more than I needed to zing his musical naiveté however.

"I might have heard of him, yeah," I said.

That song *Flower's Grave* from the album *Alice* came on and Sam4 stared into Bethany's eyes. "This is our song," he said to me, so gross and sincere that I was forced to affect what little demeanour of reciprocal sincerity I could manage. He didn't seem to care if this embarrassed Bethany. It didn't even seem like Bethany cared that this embarrassed Bethany.

"Nice sunglasses," said Bethany. It was a polite way of saying, 'Sunglasses indoors eh?'

"Thanks," I said, and tilted the sunglasses in an attempt at humour that didn't get over.

Into our third drink, which was really our sixth drink, Sam4 started to sing along to *Table Top Joe*. I have always enjoyed the physical act of singing, but from the facial responses of anyone nearby I'd slowly learned it was not an advisable practise. At twenty-two, however, it still seemed like a healthy outlet if not an outright career calling for Sam4. It's one thing to hear a recording of your own off-key voice. It's another to see a flesh and blood Photostat of yourself, possessing the same vocal chords and tonal characteristics, just hacking it up.

I interrupted Sam4's crooning by asking about the ongoing Jays game, but he was not to be interrupted. Afterwards he looked around like he was expecting applause or something. Was I this goofy? I was. I had been.

Sam4 went to his room and returned with three ecstasy tabs. He held them out with a look of mischief. It had been two days since the end of the last binge. This was enough recovery time for the strong young neurotransmitters of Sam4 and Bethany4. I could remember my own "day on/day off" schedule from the period. I was leery, but I figured ecstasy would curb further drinking and avert plate smashing for at least the first night of my vigil.

The dreary hallway began to glow in the refraction of the overhead fluorescent light cages. Only ecstasy can grace-up fluorescent lighting, I realized. Sam4 rubbed rhythmically at Bethany4's leg. That used to be my leg, I thought, bitter against all neurochemical probability; but no, I held no proprietary claim on this leg, so lithe and brown. She wasn't my Bethany. She was his Bethany. Bethany4.

The song *I'm Still Here* played with its refrain of "You haven't looked at me that way in years." I stole a look at Bethany. Her corporeal presence stood well superior to any memory constructions I'd made. There she was, content in her other-directed essence, like some saint deserving stain glass depiction. As the night wore on Bethany sat by sweetly, hands folded in lap, serotonin-enriched, occasionally contributing some passing remark. But it was clear she was a passenger in Sam4's vehicle. Despite my revulsion at seeing a me so garrulous, I could detect his appeal, especially to a young girl who didn't know better, to whom robust flakery might be mistaken for romance. She had not been loved before, making her amenable, and making her loyal, and making the inevitable betrayals that much more depressing.

Sam4 boasted of his writing career. And, lo, of his novel. I was sickened, quite sickened, but also saddened. While what Sam4 wrote that summer was sure to be utter garbage, at least he believed. Some ill-advised belief is necessary for a man to hack and claw his way past the world's other artistic aspirants. Had I believed a little longer I might have accomplished something.

Sam4 offered to read the first chapter aloud to us. Having surely endured this before, Bethany suggested he read one of his poems instead. He was adamant that nothing less than a chapter would provide the necessary insight into his creative being, so I reinforced Bethany's position by claiming I was a big poetry guy. It was a challenge to make up personal details on the spot, making this the only biographical detail I'd offered. They knew me as a man who travelled with a Bic'd head and pubic beard, wore shades indoors, and dug poesy. Sam4 read this poem:

> For those who think they're funny
> You probably are not
> For those who think they've got dignity
> We'll fuck you til you rot.

Edgy, I thought. I couldn't remember ever having written anything like that. I hoped that I had not. Bethany clapped at the end. I too clapped. Sam4 took it all in, stoic and certain of his future stature as venerated man of letters. When Sam4 busted out the second round of E Bethany declined and retired to bed. I thought it best to take a second E with my young self. We shared our philosophies on life. They were of course similar, although mine had been tempered by experience and regret. I tried to steer him towards more cautious positions. When, for example, he claimed not to fear a year or two in jail because it would provide valuable life experience, I told him that that was a stupid way to think.

He spoke of the L-S-C he'd come from and how free he felt with that shithole in the rear-view mirror. I told him that I came from Thunder Bay, another small town in northern Ontario, and could relate. We spoke of closed-mindedness and oppressive NHL worship.

"Do you think you'll ever miss them?" I asked.

I expected him to answer with bravado.

"I already miss them so much," he said.

"It doesn't get easier. If anything it gets worse," I said.

Sam4 laughed at my forthrightness, and he was me then, laughing the rueful laugh that would become the laugh most common to me.

We agreed to watch George A. Romero's original *Dawn of the Dead*. Not the standard entertainment for an ecstasy binge, but it was a film near and dear to both of our hearts. My parents had always been laissez-faire regarding the renting of R-Rated films, and Dave Reid and I had first watched it when we were only in the second grade. We'd then rented it at least twenty more times from Flambé Video before the end of elementary school.

So Sam4 and I blared the volume to hear the excellent soundtrack by Goblin. Sam4 was having such a good time that he ordered $40 worth of wings from Pizza Nova. When they came they were the kind that looked, smelled and tasted like they'd been microwaved. I always wondered why these places couldn't be up front about their microwaving of wings and encourage the consumer to microwave the wings themselves.

Needless to say they paled in comparison to Fred's Fried Chicken. I knew Sam4 was trying to recreate the Fred's/*Dawn* parties shared with Reeder during the first few years of high school. The final time Reeder had been over to my house, in grade eleven, was for a Fred's/*Dawn* experience, it might be worth noting.

Sam4 was assuredly even that moment casting me in the Reeder role. God knows I'd auditioned at least a dozen potential Reeders and came up wanting during my own early twenties. It was touching that Sam4 still thought it possible. Just as he possessed the idealism to believe in his garbage novel, so too could he believe in the emergence of a Dave Reid replacement.

"I used to watch this all the time with my buddy Dave," said Sam4.

"Yeah," I said.

"That reminds me of this essay on friendship I wrote for my Philosophy of Love and Sex class," said Sam4.

I knew all about that essay. I'd been notorious for referencing my own version during my nights at Endocrine, as though I were a world-class thinker and not some serial regurgitator and occasional plagiarist. Sam4 went to his room and returned with not one but two copies of the work in question. I feared he would read the whole thing aloud to me, but he only handed me a copy for my perusal. Its title was *The Sadness of Friendship in Aristotle's Nicomachean Ethics.* I immediately recognized the avant-garde formatting. Sam4 had given me the graded copy, a D minus. The teacher had notated, "Some good ideas but what's with this structure? Be more serious."

Some segments were in 22-point font for no discernible reason. I guess as like an underscoring of their brilliance. It all struck me as very stupid. To his credit, Sam4 had cherry-picked some of Aristotle's choice lines on friendship. He's also stripped them of all possible context. I could recall cherry-picking and context-stripping the same ones.

"Friendship stimulates those in the prime of life to noble action," quoted Sam4. "It helps the young to keep from error."

"Yeah, I'd say I was unstimulated in this regard, and it did lead to ignoble action, and much error," I offered.

"For without friends, no man would choose to live," he again quoted. "With friends men are more able to think and act."

It was true. Sam4 wouldn't be so silly if his thoughts and actions had been regulated by some good old regressive L-S-C peers. Sam4's flighty dilettantism would have been offset by his drive for social acceptance, and he'd have maybe reached some golden mean of respectable eccentricity.

"I really shouldn't care that much, but I can't stop having these dreams about Dave Reid, that asshole," he said.

I picked up the essay. "'Each loves what is good for himself,' says Aristotle here. Maybe you weren't good for Dave Reid."

"What?"

"Not everything seems to be loved, only the lovable," I said, pointing to the words on the page.

"I have always been lovable," said Sam4.

"I'm sure you are lovable, but maybe not in that time and place. Not under those circumstances. Here—you talk about 'like' people being friends, maybe you weren't 'like' this Dave Reid fellow at the time he lost interest."

"From different tunes come the fairest tones," countered Sam4, "And here it talks about beneficence, you know what beneficence means?"

"I do."

"So even if we weren't so equal in virtue, couldn't he have been beneficent until we were? Wasn't his role as virtuous friend to want the best for me?" asked Sam4.

"He was a teenager. Most teens aren't very beneficent."

"You done with this shit?" asked Sam4, referring to the wings.

I'd only gotten two down, but I was. He buried them at the bottom of the fridge where unscrupulous roommates could not find and re-microwave them.

One such roommate, Marty, came home. It was nearly 3 am so he must have been up to something other than job searching. He bought an E off Sam4 for fifteen dollars. Sam4 sure wasn't giving Marty any kind of roommate discount. Marty began furiously cleaning the kitchen, which seemed like a positive enough contribution. Then he asked Sam4 if he could buy a bag of popcorn off him.

Sam4 said, "Just take one, geez."

We all shared the bag, but I guess Marty really needed

like a whole bag of corn to himself, because after he offered to buy a second bag for a dollar. Sam4 accepted the Loonie. I suspect not so much because he wanted the money as to curb Marty's freeloading.

Having reached an unspoken accord that Marty was an oppressive presence, Sam4 and I took a walk around the block. We saw Chinatown waking up. The lawns that were allowed to grow. The bent old Tai Chi men.

"I've always loved this neighbourhood," I said.

I picked up a *Toronto Star* to catch up on the 2004 happenings. Canada was in the middle of a federal election. It was as boring now as it had been the first time around. I saw that former Liberal Prime Minister Paul Martin was now named Paul Morrissey however, and looked just like the foppish singer-songwriter Morrissey.

Back in the apartment Marty scanned the classifieds for work. He found a listing for a lathe-man. Since I'd bought the paper he declared me a good omen. Sam4 latched onto this and began speaking in quasi-mystical terms. He produced a copy of *The Celestine Prophecy* and told me how vital it would be to my personal development. He demanded that I read it, like that minute, like stop interacting with him and Marty, sit myself down and read the book cover to cover and then get back to him, he'd be waiting. I promised to read it the next day. I'd read the book at the same time in my life as Sam4 had, and in subsequent years I'd come to recognize it as the worst type of flim-flammery. Sam4 then suggested he'd wake Bethany to engage her in some *Celestine Prophecy*-related discussion, as she too had been assigned to read it.

"Let her sleep," I said.

I told Sam4 I was heading to bed myself, though I was wired as all-get-out and knew I'd be up for hours.

"Let me read you another poem," he said, "That other one isn't my best."

"Maybe tomorrow."

"Come on Steve," he said, "It's called *A Few Words About Teddy.*"

"Okay."

He stood before me on the couch, like a damned serious orator.

> *We'll miss you Teddy*
> *Is written in marker*
> *On a city park bench*
> *This glorious eulogy*
> *Simple and true*
> *Has not been cleaned by park staff*
> *They'd seen Teddy around.*
>
> *For Teddy sat there*
> *Drinking his Max Ice*
> *In the good years*
> *And choking back Listerine near the end*
> *Talking with friends so wonderful*
> *Over the morning's first bottle*
> *Head drooping at night*
> *Risking pneumonia, too drunk*
> *To make it to the shelter*
>
> *We hope Teddy is in his heaven now*
> *With a bottomless bottle of Heineken*
> *That never makes him sleepy or stupid*
> *But fills him with the happiness he so loved*
> *Of the morning's first drink forever!*

22

It took fourteen hours of staring at the ceiling before sleep came. I got a Pita from Pita Pit because I needed some goddamn nutrients, but then I got all savoury toppings like olives and pickles on top of a gyro which is like crispy fried lamb so all things considered it wasn't healthy at all.

I decided to check on Sam1. I walked the couple blocks to the rooming house at College and Spadina. When I knocked on his door I heard some unholy hybrid of slurred curses and screaming.

"Faaaugaau," would be a rough onomatopoeic translation.

"Open the door Sam1."

The door swung open to reveal Sam1 lying bloody on the floor. Blood was everywhere; on his sheets, the curtains, on his two (!) empty 60s of vodka.

"Sam1, this is quite the bad scene," I said.

"Fucker stabbed me," said Sam1, nowhere near that clearly, but I will not burden the reader with further onomatopoeic interpretation.

A flap of skin hung down from Sam1's right bicep.

"Did he get you anywhere else?"

Sam1 only looked sullenly at the floor, so I lifted his t-shirt to check the torso, home to most of a man's vital organs.

"How long have you been bleeding like this for?" I asked.

Sam1 didn't have an answer. I found myself in a quandary. He might have required an immediate hospital visit, but without a health card, sure to warrant attention from the police, that could set Sam1 up for an indefinite visit to the Don Jail.

I had to stop the bleeding with some kind of tourniquet. Sam1 was wearing his only clothes. I was wearing my only clothes. There was one stained sheet on the bed, probably a real hot zone of bacterias up to and not improbably containing downright deadly Philoviruses. I ended up wadding up a bunch of it and pressing it against Sam1's wound.

"Hold that there," I told him. "Do you remember who stabbed you?"

"Neighbour."

I needed to know how long he'd been bleeding for. Jail would be bad for Sam1, bleeding out would be worse. I walked down the hall and shouted, "Can anyone tell me how long ago the tenant in 301 was stabbed please?"

Silence.

"I'm not calling the police. I just need to know so I can take him to the hospital if necessary."

"About fifteen minutes ago," a man said from behind his door, most likely the stabber.

I could live with that. Sam1 would have enough blood for the next few minutes. At a Shopper's Drug Mart I bought a water bottle, rubbing alcohol, a first aid kit that contained a needle and thread, and a large tensor bandage. I had never stitched anyone up before. Nor had I sewn before. Exactly the type of scenario that tutorials on YouTube were made for. I wasn't far from the library and debated a quick log-in to learn about stitching, but figured a crude stitch-job would be less taxing for Sam1 than death by bleedout. When I got back to the room Sam1 was passed out, but not dead, only sleeping.

"This is going to hurt," I said, unpacking my purchases.

"I need a drink first," Sam1 said.

"You have exhausted your supplies."

Sam1 eyed the Isopropyl.

"No, that's a low you should not sink to."

"I'll need it," he said.

I considered my inexperience with sewing. I glanced at his bloody flap of bicep. I passed him the Isopropyl and watched in horror as he gulped half of it down.

"Around 2024," he said, "I used to drink this stuff all the time."

I poured water and the rest of the alcohol over the wound. Sewing shut a wound, I would learn, requires sure, confident motions, and it took many failed needle penetrations before I developed the necessary economy of movement. Always having lacked fine motor skills, it was tying the knot at the end I feared most. I fumbled with the needles for a solid two minutes, rubbing dirty thumbs and index fingers that I'd forgotten to wash into his wound, undoing any disinfectant good accomplished by the rubbing alcohol. Finally I made the tiny knot. Sam1 fell asleep.

I'd been unwilling to leave my $4000 in cash in my room at Sam4's because of the flimsy lock. I noticed a Ziploc bag with some remnants of white powder in it. I opened the toilet tank. I did a quick empty-bagged test to determine if flushing the toilet would suck my wad into shit-filled sewers, determined that flushing would not, stuck my money in the bag and replaced the lid.

I bought a forty-ounce bottle of vodka and a case of soda and put them by Sam1's bed. It might lead him to more trouble, but he was going to need it. I sat on his bed until deciding that this was a depressing way to spend an afternoon, especially while on vacation from Newtonian principles and all. I went back to Sam4's apartment, smoked weed with Marty and listened to Marty tell me about his experience in the military for an honest-to-God three hours.

When Marty left for one of his 'job interviews' I put my ear up to Sam4's door and heard nothing. I knocked. No one answered. I dickied Sam4's door with the intention of using the Internet on his big black Dell PC.

An MSN message from Nicole4 flashed in the bottom right corner of his monitor.

"Oh My God I'm so sorry to message you out of the blue like this but I just found this amazing condo for rent and I just went ahead and got my dad to wire me the down payment but I have no one to help me move on the 1st because everyone is gone for the summer, well just my roommate but she's tiny like me. I know this is out of nowhere but please please please I'll buy you beer and even give you a little money if you want and pizza or whatever when we're done but we're too little to carry a couch by ourselves."

The previous message from Nicole4 had been sent a calendar year earlier. It was the word "No," in response to Sam4's query, "Up for hanging out tonight?" This was low. This was the power that friend-zoning little person had held over me, over Sam1, over Sam4, over all of us but that charming dickens Sam3.

Sam1 and I had precious little to occupy our time on this worldline, as evidenced by Sam1's more destructive proclivities getting the better of him and resulting in his stabbing. Peeved by her presumptuousness though I was, it always made me happy to be in Nicole's presence, even if it was in the chilly shadow of the friend zone. Perhaps I am a born cuckold.

I wrote back, "Hey Nicole, afraid I'm going to be out of town. As luck would have it my uncle and my cousin whom you've never met are staying at my place right now, and they are Quakers, which involves doing a lot of good deeds. They can definitely help you."

She wrote back, "They aren't weird are they?"

"Totally normal, Nicole. They even look just like me."

"Aww, serious cuties then," she wrote.

She gave an address, a time of 11 am, and a date that was two days away. I went to tell Sam1, but Sam1 was passed out, so I left him a note. I figured if he had something to look forward to it would prevent him from getting his guts carved out in the interim.

I woke to the festive sounds of Tom Waits and popcorn popping. I sat beside Marty on the couch and helped myself to a handful. I wasn't sure of the protocol. Maybe I was supposed to give Marty a dime per handful, or .25 cents per quarter bag. Marty wasn't exactly passing me the bag, and I had to maneuver my hand over his for each helping. It was in this scenario, mooching already-mooched microwaved popcorn from Marty, that I almost missed the event I was there to prevent.

The young couple weren't yelling or gesticulating with any notable fervour. They spoke quietly over the dish sink. The great curse of the Sam McQuiggan experience is the ability to drink a great deal without appearing drunk. I had worked eight hour shifts while blind drunk, interacting with managers and clients, and no one had wised up. Or perhaps in some cases the managers and clients had preferred to appear unwise. It's a hell of a thing, exposing someone's secret drinking problem. Point is, a civilian would not have recognized Sam4 as drunk, but I detected the slightest bob to his skull, a waviness about the face, a haze of hate emanating from the upper chakras.

His hand waved into the sink, looking for purchase. I moved quicker than I had any physiological right to, cutting down on my time by sliding the last three feet across the linoleum floor to a position directly between Sam4 and Bethany4.

"Can I help you?" asked Sam4.

"No, but I think I can help you," I said. "Come to my room."

"Why?" asked Sam4.

"I scored some great acid."

Sam4 had told me that acid was the one drug lacking in the Toronto rave scene. It was his white whale. I had no acid, requiring this big pantomime of, "Oh shit, where did it go?" and "Man, fifty tabs, how could I have…." Sam4 was so hungry for psychonautical nourishment that he got down on hands and knees with me for twenty minutes until we gave up. No plates were smashed, what rage that raised the plate had subsided, and Sam4 sat beside Marty and me on the couch and nursed a restorative Corona, the Gatorade of the hard-drinking man.

Though the mission was accomplished, I did not feel wholly satisfied. It was not unlike writing one's last exam at university. A type of "What now, then?" feeling. I could go and tell Sam1 that our mission was a success worth celebrating given the murderous debacle we'd perpetrated on Sam3's worldline. But then what? Back to my worldline? To a condo I might no longer own, a life of loneliness and pathetic longing, a life without even a Bethany4 nearby to ease the pain? I rationalized. One plate smashing having been averted wouldn't protect future plates and bowls from Sam4's anger.

I wanted to stay. I had nowhere better to go and nothing better to be. I asked Sam4 if he wanted to go to Endocrine on the weekend. He said that he did.

I went outside and took a big breath before remembering the sulphuric atmosphere. I coughed and almost vomited. This brought to mind a line from a Denis Johnson book about belonging in hell. Since I had nothing better to do I walked to the Lillian H. Smith library and looked it up.

"He decided to go over a couple of blocks to Michael's Tavern for something cold, and as he walked beside the road he felt his anger burning up in the heat of noon, and saw himself, as he often did when he was outdoors on hot days, being forged in enormous fires for some purpose beyond his imagining. He was only walking down a street toward a barroom, and yet in his own mind he took his part in the eternity of this place. It seemed to him—it was not the first time—that he belonged in Hell, and would always find himself joyful in its midst. It seemed to him that to touch James Houston was to touch one iota of the vast grit that made the desert and hid the fires at the centre of the earth."

I had been raised Catholic, and though my faith had lapsed, the fear of hell is something that sticks with a man. An unwelcome thought seized me. Maybe I was that very minute descending into hell. All bets were off once you perverted the space-time continuum, known in some circles as "God's perfect creation," and maybe each jump, each transgression against the natural order, reserved for me an extra eon or two of anguish in the pit.

I had no one to discuss this concern with other than Sam1 When I got to his room he was lying face down on his mattress and moaning.

"It's all gone," he said.

"What is?"

"All my money."

"How?" I asked.

"First a card game, then crack, then some crack prostitutes, and it was my association with them, the crack prostitutes, that led to the robbery," said Sam1.

"Sam1, I would be remiss if I didn't say that you brought this upon yourself."

"All I've got left is this," he said, holding up his keys and his long-term parking ticket from Pearson Airport.

I looked for my Ziploc bag of money in the toilet. The robbers had known all the angles. My money was gone. I was down to the $200 I'd kept in my wallet.

"How much do you have left?" asked Sam1.

"None," I lied, "I stashed all of mine in your toilet tank."

"Oh for fuck fucking sake," said Sam1, starting to bawl.

Finding this awkward, I walked around the block, came back, and told him we might make some money helping Nicole move the next day, or at least get some food and free beer out of it.

"So we make $50 at the most. How long does that last us?" said Sam1.

"Maybe contact with one of the Nicole's will do you some spiritual good. Go rest up. We have about twenty hours," I said.

I returned to McCaul Street because it was less depressing than listening to Sam1 whimper about what a screw-up he was. I found Sam4 in the alley behind the apartment washing his flip flops in a bucket. He appeared in relatively good spirits. I figured it was as good a time as any to proposition him.

"Sam4," I began, and realized my blunder. "Sam for years I've wanted to get in the drug game. I see you have a fine trade going. I would like to buy in. I will not horn in on your turf. You can believe that. Your turf will be left to you entirely."

"$10 a pill if you buy at least ten pills," he said.

"I was thinking $7.25."

"I pay $8."

"You pay $7," I said.

"How do you know that?"

"Someone told me at The Womb."

"I've got to keep my mouth shut," said Sam4. "Fine, $8 then. I still need to make a profit on this, and you need to buy at least twenty to get the $8 rate. You see how I'm only making $20 and there was the risk involved in picking these up in the first place."

$160 would leave me with $40 to my name, to say nothing of what would be left to Sam1's name. On the other hand, one night at Endocrine and I could turn that $160 into $300 or $400.

"It's a deal," I said.

"Don't tell Marty how much I sold them to you for."

"Okay."

"And don't undercut me with Marty."

"What are you guys talking about?" asked Marty through the apartment's small rear window, also its only window.

"Popcorn," I said.

Sam4 started laughing so hard that he almost fell into a bunch of garbage cans, and again I saw some good in the young man.

····· 24 ·····

In the morning I was surprised to find a container of Ginger Beef in the fridge that Marty had not yet gotten to. It looked soggy and unappetizing, but I expected to find Sam1 in a state of ill health that could only be rectified by protein, water, and the passage of time. I found nothing of the sort. The door was unlocked and inside Sam1 was doing sit-ups on his bed.

"You're looking hale," I said.

"I have turned over a new leaf Sam2. I have experienced a wake-up call."

I considered it polite not to ask how many wake up calls Sam1 had responded to in his life.

"Ginger Beef?" I asked

"Already ate," he said.

"You found some money?"

"No, there's like a coffee hour after mass at St. Michael's. I went a little hard on the muffins, but no one seemed to mind. They were happy to see a new face."

"Church already?"

"Yes sir, mass at eight this morning and an AA meeting last night at nine."

"Good for you, Sam1. Should we head over to Nicole's?"

"Before we go I want to make clear that, in line with AA principles, I'm doing this for altruistic purposes, as an act of penance as it were, and not for any lecherous contact with Nicole4 that might be motivating you, though, also as a tenet of my recovery, I am not judging you for any lechery-related motivations you might be cursed by."

"Superlative," I said.

It was amazing how you could go from the rooming house to the eighteenth century architecture of UofT in just a couple blocks. The birds were singing. Summer students were rushing towards classes and futures. It was enough to make a time travellin' man yearn for a second chance.

Nicole4 awaited us at the door. I noticed the best divergence yet. On this worldline Nicole4 had a world-class rack! And though she was still petite, Nicole's breasts weren't fake, you could just tell by the dynamics of a fatty jiggle detectable when she jumped up and down in a faux-enthusiastic greeting of Sam1 and me.

My sunglasses were wholly appropriate outdoors. She hadn't seen Sam in at least a year, making a shaved head conceivable. She wasn't presented with any cognitive dissonance because the real Sam4 wasn't in the vicinity. She came to the reasonable conclusion I'd been expecting someone to reach ever since I'd arrived on this worldline.

"Sam, you made it after all," she said.

"Hey," said I.

"You look so much older!" she squealed.

"This is my Uncle Doug, from the Northwest Territories," I said.

Sam1 gave me an ugly look. I hoped his new code of honour wouldn't stand in my way. Deceiving Nicole4 couldn't be approved of by the pals of Bill W.

"My roommate Bella is going to be here with the truck any minute," said Nicole4. "Maybe you guys can start taking apart the bed."

I'd thought we were muscle only. Strictly carrying duty. Turned out we were providing all the services a typical boyfriend or family member might. Naturally I wasn't very good with a tool kit, so it fell on Uncle Doug to unscrew the thousand-odd pieces of Nicole4's Ikea bedframe.

"What have you been up to?" she asked me.

"Just chilling," I responded.

"Like a villain," she said.

I had forgotten this insipid turn of phrase.

Bella arrived. She was an emo cartoon with many facial

piercings, weighing about eighty-five pounds. I had a hunch. On my worldline, on all the worldlines where Nicole remained flat-chested, it was waifish Bella who was well-endowed, like there was some cosmic balance wherein only one of these roommates could have great tits. There was no way to prove it. I just knew.

Bella began playing A Simple Plan on her laptop. I had also forgotten the pop punk revolution of the early 2000s. It was amusing that Bella's entire dark and pierced aesthetic owed itself to such a fleeting commercial fad. I was wondering if she had any regrettable tattoos when she bent over to reveal a Good Charlotte tramp stamp. Tramp stamps were another fashion that history would not favour. No one I knew called them such in 2004. They were just back tattoos to us then. They were considered sexy, or at least a signifier of *the sexual*, in the circles I ran in anyway. I often wonder what all the tramp-stamped but otherwise classy girls think about this change in the narrative. I could picture Bella in 2016 working at some big actuarial firm or something, always at serious pains to hide her trampish and youthful enthusiasm for Good Charlotte.

I'll not detail the slapstick montage full of couches not quite fitting through doors, a mattress cascading down a flight of stairs and nearly maiming Uncle Doug, and Uncle Doug farting so heinously and so often that Bella made a big show of plugging her nose. The overriding theme of the day involved the entitlement of sexy petite youth. For example, there were many boxes of clothes the girls could have easily carried that fell on Uncle Doug and me to cart down. They just stood around talking. In subsequent years they would have been glued to their phones. It proved to me that phones had not made us, as a species, assholes. We'd always been assholes.

When we arrived at Nicole4's new condo it looked like it would have been a bit too swanky for Patrick Bateman himself. Fortunately there was a whole concierge team eager to help us with our carrying responsibilities. After the first few loads Nicole offered to get takeout.

"What do you guys want?" she said.

"Red Lobster," I said.

"The Keg," said Uncle Doug.

"Which one?"

"Both," said Uncle Doug.

"Okay…" Nicole said in that injured way she was so good at.

A half hour later Nicole returned with takeout from The Keg only.

"No Red Lobster nearby," she said.

She also had a bottle of Smirnoff and a four-pack of good Guinness beer. Uncle Doug eyed the liquid supplies with hunger, but managed to placate himself by digging into a steak sandwich gone soggy. I tried to remember if Nicole had ever drank beer or if this was a divergence. It didn't matter. By the second one she was drunk and resting her head against my chest on the couch. Bella had retired to her new room to blare some Coldplay, considered the apex of fine musical taste at the time.

When Nicole went to the bathroom Uncle Doug asked me if I was ready to leave. I told Uncle Doug that I was content where I was for the time being. He borrowed Nicole's key fob and went to sit by the outdoor pool and reflect on his serenity or something.

"I can't believe how much older you look," Nicole said.

"Time will do that to a man," I said.

"You're so funny!" she shrieked. "Take off your sunglasses."

She recoiled in shock.

"Whoa, you really do look way, way older. I can't even believe it. What have you been eating?"

"Spinach," I said.

She shrieked again.

"Let's do a shot," I said.

We each did two.

"I didn't get a chance to see your room," I said.

This was the type of assertive move that I had never been capable of as a young Sam2, but age and hate and a paucity of fucks given about consequences on this worldline had hardened my resolve. She led me by the hand into the bedroom and flopped down on her bed.

"Feel how soft it is," she said.

I positioned myself on top of her and kissed her.

"Oh Sam, I never thought you had it in you. You used to seem like a little boy."

We grinded for a while. One of the things I miss most about youth is grinding. Pants were removed and it became apparent that insertion was expected. Perhaps owing to the pressure of fulfilling a lifelong goal, or more likely to the recent wear and tear inflicted on my nervous system, initial insertion attempts were less than fruitful.

"Maybe next time," she said.

I appeared stoic. I tried to kiss her again but she was through with me and returned to the living room. Uncle Doug had returned from the pool. He hadn't been dressed for the pool anyway.

"So Sam2, I mean so Sam today mentioned you might give us some cash. I hate to ask but I'm really low on funds," said Uncle Doug.

After the impotency fiasco this was about the most embarrassing thing he could have said. Nicole handed three twenties to Uncle Doug along with some silence.

"That's it for both of us?" asked Uncle Doug.

"You take it Uncle Doug. I'm doing just great financially," I said.

Uncle Doug laughed.

"It was so nice seeing you," Nicole said, and hugged me.

"Oh fuck you," I said.

··· ·····
··· :····
····· :··· ·····

I returned to McCaul street so tired from the day's toil that I'd completely forgotten it was the big night out at Endocrine. My first reminder was an aural one, with DJ Tiesto blaring loud enough for me to hear from two houses away.

Sam4 greeted me with a hug of nearly a minute's duration. I took the opportunity to also hug Bethany4. Bethany4 was wearing a tank-top with a built-in bra contraption. It was either heavily padded or she too was enjoying some minor version of the bustline-divergence that had improved upon Nicole4's bust. Marty was mopping the kitchen floor like the fate of mankind hung in the balance. This was something of a hindrance to the dozen assembled rank strangers to me who were trying to dance on the kitchen floor.

I decided to chew my first ecstasy tab for more expedient results. As I was washing the acrid taste off my tongue with a Corona, Sam4 announced that it was time to go. He handed Bethany4 his baggy of pills to stuff in her bra. As exploitive as it seemed, it really was the smart play. The bouncers checked pockets, shoes, underneath hats, but they would not broach the sexed-up sanctity of a young woman's bra. I didn't want to encroach on Bethany4's built-in bra in this way either, considering its storage capacity a boyfriend-specific privilege.

"What do you think's safer?" I asked the crowd, "The very front of my shoe, or the old tinfoil package in the rectum?"

"I can take yours too," Bethany4 said.

"Gee, thanks Bethany."

We stepped out into one of the freshest summer nights that existence may ever have manifested, leaving Marty to scrub the ceilings, do pushups, and read back issues of *Lathe-Man Quarterly* for all we knew.

Sam4 walked ahead with his guests. Bethany4 fell back to walk with me. Here was her care-giving nature laid bare. She was willing to forego fun with her friends to hang out with a strange new roommate who might have otherwise felt excluded. I smiled at her, but the smile must have looked like a terrifying grimace because I was already grinding my teeth.

"Sam should have warned you," she said, "The E he got this time is way way stronger."

I squeezed her shoulders.

"Why do you wear those sunglasses all the time? It's night time. Isn't it hard to see?"

"Allergic to light," I said, not sure if I intended this as a joke or not.

She didn't press further. Also under the auspices of strong E, she poured out her personal history, most of it very similar to the personal history of my Bethany: her childhood Girl Guide exploits, her misguided enthusiasm for Blink 182, the come-backer that had nearly blinded her in an eighth grade softball experience. Then she spoke of meeting Sam, and it killed me, because it was the same way she'd met me, free of divergence.

"I love him so much," she said.

"I'm sure he feels the same way," I said, but then my statement was made to seem dubious when Sam4 placed his arms around the sizable waists of two older Brazilian women in the entourage.

We entered Endocrine at the perfect time, with the beat in one of those periods of hyper-fast repetition. I bobbed my head as rapidly as my neck would allow. Sam4 again hugged me and asked if I needed any E, having forgotten that he'd sold me a bunch of E and that I had joined him on the sales and distribution side of the Endocrine E economy.

Bethany4 came out of the bathroom and handed us our bags of pills. Sam4 hugged both of us at the same time. When he left to circulate the club I chose to sit with Bethany4. It was difficult to talk over the noise so we mostly bobbed our heads. I enjoyed this period of syncopated bobbing with her.

I gave Bethany4 a solid fifteen-minute massage. Sam4 walked by and seemed cool with the tactile exchange. Massaging another dude's girlfriend was par for the course at these pill-happy events. As were light shows. Some loser came by and offered us one. I tried to decline, but Bethany4 was too kind to refuse and this guy waved glow sticks in our faces for a forty-five second period that felt more like a week.

"Let me wear your sunglasses," Bethany4 yelled at me.

"No."

Just as she plucked them off my face the music entered a new ethereal phase and a bright white light soaked the venue.

"What the hell?" she said, placing her index finger on the freckle by my eye.

Where was lightshow Don to offer distraction when you needed him?

"What's going on?" she asked.

There was no recourse but for the truth.

"I'm a time traveler," I yelled over the music.

"What?" she yelled.

"I'm a time traveler," I yelled.

"I can't hear you," she yelled.

"Let's go outside," I yelled, and led her by the hand to the not-so-fresh air outside Endocrine.

"Hey Sam," said Leafs Jersey.

Bethany4 shivered.

"I need to go home. I'm too high right now," she said.

"You're not high," I said, "Well, you are high, but you aren't hallucinating. I am a future version of Sam. No, I am just Sam. A different Sam. But the same Sam."

Bethany4 started crying and looked more beautiful than any recollection I owned of her. I'd taken a second E about twenty minutes earlier, swallowing it whole this time. It was kicking in at, given the centuries of torture I'd go on to endure, an altogether unfortunate moment.

"I'm here to save you Bethany," I said, the details coming together as my synapses fired with lightning speed.

"What are you talking about?"

"Tomorrow, you and Sam go to an after party, and you will overdose on GHB. Sam never forgives himself."

This was good. This was persuasive.

"How do you know?" she asked.

"Because it happened to me."

At this point the words "the latitude, the latitude, the latitude," were repeating endlessly from the club. To my addled brain this seemed some cosmic message about inter-temporal voyaging.

"Why are they talking about latitude?" I asked.

"She's saying *attitude.* Madonna is," Bethany4 said.

"You have to come with me," I said.

"I can't leave him."

I knew then that I had her. I'd always been able to steamroll over her better instincts by playing on her maternal protection instinct. The basic formula had been, "What I may be doing is stupid, but I'm going to do it anyway, and I'm going to need your support." All while hinting at some grander vision only I could access. "You'll have to trust me"-type thing. I looked at her sadly and sincerely and said:

"Listen Bethany, if you leave him now it will suck for him tomorrow, and for the next few months, but he'll get over it. If you stay, and what happens happens, he'll never be the same. Because it will be his fault. Trust me. I know. I lost you. That's why I'm here."

"I just won't take any G. I won't go to the after party," she said.

"It doesn't work like that," I said, "The winds of fate cannot be unblown."

This was not so good. This was perhaps not so persuasive.

Prompt action was in order. I took her arm and started running in the direction of Queen Street, pretending we were in an action film, knowing she had always enjoyed action films.

"Where are we going?" she asked.

"To my time machine," I yelled, and pointed an index finger skyward for effect.

"What about Sam?" she asked.

"I am Sam," I again yelled. "Not like the retard movie, though."

She didn't laugh.

"But you're so much older," she said.

"I'm more mature, less of an asshole. I'll be able to appreciate you. Treat you the way you deserve. I know it might seem like a tough sell. But it's either no life with him, or a life with me. And I'm him, get it?"

"You look older," she said again.

"I can start moisturizing."

"I had a dream that you were Sam, right when you first came," Bethany4 said.

"Again, the machinations of fate. We have a stressful journey ahead of us. I think you should take this," I said, and handed her an E. She considered and then swallowed the E.

"What about my stuff?"

"How much do you weigh?" I asked.

"Why?"

"Time machine weight limits, though they do seem to be somewhat amorphous, not exactly pinned down."

"One-thirty."

"Okay, you can bring ten pounds worth of stuff."

"When are we going? Boy that sounds weird," she said.

"Would you prefer the future or the past?"

She shrugged.

It dawned on me that I was once more planning on jumping through time, what Khalid Masood considers, "the highest form of matter," with exactly jack shit for a plan.

We stopped at the apartment and Bethany4 picked up a picture album and a few pairs of clothes.

"Will it be summer or winter?" she asked, "And is this a hallucination? I did some ketamine earlier."

"It isn't the K," I said, "It can be whatever season we want. Let's aim for summer. And is there any more K?"

We each did a line of K. I put on that album *Kid A* by Radiohead. Bethany2 and I had enjoyed some beatific periods of drug-enhanced affection to that album. I knew it would work for any Bethany and any Sam in this sad old multiverse. We started kissing. She had always been a very sweet kisser. I felt this big surge of dopamine and pulled her closer to me. There was a solid two minute stretch where we just pressed our lips together without moving and stared into each other's eyes. That cemented it somehow. I was me. She was no longer Bethany4 but just Bethany, my Bethany again.

"You really are Sam," she said.

"I have missed you so much Bethany," I said.

She wrote Sam a note that read, "I love you Sam but I have to leave for reasons that can't be explained. Tell my parents I love them and not to worry. I am safe. I'm not just high and crazy trust me. I love you so much Sam."

I felt a pang of remorse. The plates had gone unsmashed, but I'd sure left Sam4 in a bad way. He'd be coming down to this nightmare, and would not be well-equipped to deal with any forthcoming missing person investigation.

We took a cab to the rooming house. I picked up a large stone outside, the plan being to bonk Sam1 and steal his keys and parking pass. This went against my drugged-up condition, but I was a slave to a new drug, a drug that was going to last. Happily, the rock didn't end up being necessary. His door was unlocked and slightly ajar, perhaps to encourage down-on-their-luck neighbours to visit for some spiritual counsel. He was on his bed reading the King James Bible. His jeans were folded on a chair by the door. I opened the door, grabbed the jeans, grabbed the parking ticket and keys from the left pocket, and ran. Sam1 stuck his head out the door just as I hit the stairs, but did not chase, perhaps owing to a paucity of pants, or general world-weariness, or even more likely as a last act of penance for his lifetime of shitty behaviour.

"What in the hell are you doing?" were the last words I'd

hear from Sam1.

"Will my parents be there, the time and place we're going?" Bethany asked in the cab.

"Yes, but there will be another you, and your parents will consider that you to be you, so it's up to you if you want to impose on them or not."

I regretted what I'd said, not only because I'd used the word *you* five times, but because I didn't want to queer the deal and lose this Bethany, so close to being mine again thanks to our current surpluses of serotonin and a watershed album by the finest musical act of the 21st century.

We got to the van and I set the controls for 2016, as good a time as any. Even with a 10+% divergence I could make some money on sports gambling. I could work under the table if necessary. I would find a way. The location setting of the High Park baseball field would be as good in 2016 as it was for 2004, so I let it be.

"Let's blow this popsicle stand," I said, continuing with the action movie theme, "And by popsicle stand I mean worldline!"

"I don't even know what's going on anymore," said Bethany.

Before she could reconsider I positioned her on top of me on the TDU's lone groove. It felt good to be on the bottom, not to have Sam1's junk pressed into me. The friction with Bethany was altogether more pleasant. I touched the contents of her built-in bra. I kissed her neck. I moved her up a little bit and despite the ravages of E on the libido, nervous system, and all other boner-producing agents, we managed to make love for the first thirty minutes of our journey, lovers in time, as it were. Afterwards our E started to wear off and we were thirsty as the occupants of hell. What waited was a pit of uncertainty. But I'd done it. I'd reconciled the great error of my life. I'd stolen Bethany back from the past.

Then the machine started to rattle and hum. It was kicking into a higher gear. I looked at the temporametre for the first time. It wasn't moving forwards but backwards. And with this new boost in power it was suddenly moving at a speed of one-hundred years a minute instead of one year an hour.

"Uh-oh," I said.

"What?"

"Uh, nothing."

As the machine started to slow down, an enormous force rattled our bodies, causing Bethany to hit her head on the roof of the TDU. Then came a stillness. I opened the TDU's door and saw the van's windows had been shattered, either by an increase in the TDU's radioactive emissions or by the external environment we'd entered.

Tactile sensation makes for dubious input at the best of times, but within the context of time it is all but meaningless. What I initially detected as a breeze coming in through the window, within a split-second, soon became the coldest cold I'd ever felt. It was -75 Celsius at least.

The divergence meter read 386.4%. That was not good. I looked at the landscape. It was much redder than the world-lines we'd known in that it was a florid magenta. The sky too was dissimilar in that it was the yellow of pus or old ejaculate. I squeezed Bethany for warmth.

"I knew this was a bad idea," she said.

Of all the letdowns Sam4 had perpetrated upon her, all

the after-parties she'd been abandoned at, all the drunken re-
marks that had embarrassed her, I could be sure he had not
brought her to an uninhabitable world.

"Something must have went wrong. Let's just jump back
to the old worldline. I think the settings for that one are still
here in the Recent History tab," I said.

"How many times have you done this before?"

"First time actually."

The moment I pressed the touch-screen I received a
Please Restart prompt. I clicked Okay.

Restarting 1%.

A minute went by and it still said 1%. Bethany had little
to say to me.

"Sure looks red out there," I said.

After fifteen minutes it still said Restarting 1% and thirst
began to trump our patience.

"Try restarting again," said Bethany.

"Maybe it takes a long time to restart, like each percent
takes a half hour, so by trying again we'd lose the time already
invested. And my body temperature is dropping fast."

"Let's try restarting one more time. Maybe it will work."

I hit restart and for another ten minutes it was stuck on
1%.

"We need to find some water," said Bethany.

A part of me saw her taking charge as a blow to my
manliness; on the other hand I've never been fond of excessive
responsibility.

"It's too cold out," I observed.

"Let's run like a hundred yards just to see," said Bethany,
"It can't be much colder than in here."

We ran. The ground had the consistency and sheen of a
consumer electronic, a speaker or a router, for example, only

in the aforementioned shade of magenta. We saw some bubbling liquid in a concavity.

"Maybe that is the water of this earth," I said.

"It looks more like lava."

You could feel the heat from several feet away, so we figured, 'Yeah, probably lava.'

"At least we can warm our hands over it," I said.

Some horrendous bird with the head of a pig scuttled by. Thirst is a powerful motivator, and I thought to kill the bird-pig so as to drink its blood. This might have also improved my standing as a provider with Bethany. I tackled the bird-pig and began punching its skull. I tried to snap its neck but the neck was hard as metal. The bird-pig trotted off, squealing out its pig scream.

"Well, that was a bust," said Bethany.

"Maybe there's some water in that cave," I said, trying to put the pig-bird fiasco behind us.

While the cave lacked water, it did have another lava pond, and provided shelter from the murderous wind.

"I guess we cower here while we wait for the machine to restart," I said.

We held each other for warmth. I had the feeling Bethany wouldn't have been in the mood to contact me were warmth not a priority.

Cloaked lizard men walked by in the distance. One of them noticed me, alerted the rest, and they took off sliding across the ground with the approximate velocity of a bobsled.

"Now that is a beautiful sight," I said to Bethany.

"Even if you've killed us," said Bethany, not without disdain, "At least I've seen things no twenty-first century woman was meant to see."

"Want to take another E?" I asked.

"Probably not, dying of dehydration."

I ran back to check on the machine. Miracle of miracles—it was at 2%. I was headed back to tell Bethany the good news when I was spotted by a gang of troglodytes. Perhaps the experience with the lizard men had imbued me with a false sense of dominance. I held myself erect and walked past them into the cave.

"Good news or bad news?" I asked Bethany.

"Good," she said.

"The TDU is at 2%."

"And the bad?"

The bad was made self-evident when the gang of troglodytes entered the mouth of the cave. I could see from the look in the lead troglodyte's eyes that it wasn't me they were interested in. I stood in front of Bethany, perhaps my most gallant act in this entire narrative, but was surprised to be pushed to the ground by a hand that extended directly out of one of the troglodyte's sternums. They were three-handed troglodytes, these.

Soon they had Bethany and were carrying her off to a probable troglodytic rape dungeon. It was a rotten position for a guy to be in, incapable of defending your new bride from the lowest order of not even Cro-Magnon man.

"Hey, hey you put her down now," I shouted.

I was on the receiving end of a withering look from Bethany when a futuristic hybrid of a bus and a sports car materialized. From it emerged a man wearing some high-tech earmuffs; a Letterman sweater, like an old college football player; and what looked like welder's glasses.

He zapped first one troglodyte and then another with some future gun that shot green rays. He was a good shot, killing six troglodytes in six shots and never coming close to hitting Bethany. The remaining few trogs lurched off in fear. The man picked Bethany up off the ground with a territorial air I did not like one bit.

"So," the man said, looking at me in exasperation, "What do you have to say for yourself?"

"Who are you?" I asked.

"I am obviously John Titor," he said.

"Yes, that does seem obvious now. Thanks for the email, by the way, back on my worldline. I should have heeded your advice and just filed a grievance against Sam1 right off the bat."

"The John Titor who sent that email has been long, long-since fired for failing so miserably at his duties. He had one job. He underestimated your Sam1, focussing most of his energy on Bruce Halverson1, whom he mistakenly assumed would cause greater temporal havoc," said John Titor.

"Why, may I ask, are you just arriving now?"

"It's easy to track a Bruce Halverson1. We can put ourselves in his shoes. His actions fit some mould of probability based on rational self-interest. With you clowns the motivations were never something our people could fathom. That made you tough to find until you travelled ten thousand years into the past. That kind of thing creates a blip on the radar. It is just not done. Maybe you can see why?"

"Can I warm up in your car?" asked Bethany.

"Sure," said John Titor. I detected a flirtatious tone.

"So what's the plan?" I asked, "And can I also sit in your car?"

"We're all getting in the vehicle," he said.

"Where to?" I asked, aiming for jovial, "And here I'm talking big picture."

"Bethany will be returned to her exact worldline," said

John Titor.

"Won't that create an untenable dual occupant scenario?" I asked.

"She'll be replacing herself. Doesn't apply," said Titor.

"What about me?"

"You will face trial. You will be punished for your grievous actions."

"Like life in prison?"

"More like half a million years in a psychic hell. The new regime does not take kindly on you early time criminals. Outside of the legal repercussions, there is the embarrassment you caused the financial interests behind TMI. It may not surprise you to learn these individuals remain free and more powerful than ever. You're lucky I found you first."

"Shit," I said.

I sat in the back seat with Bethany. I tried to squeeze her hand but she pulled it away.

"Goodbye Bethany," I said.

"Oh go to hell," she said, causing John Titor to laugh.

And that's just what I would do.

We arrived in 2061, the year this John Titor had originated from. Bethany was escorted to The Department of Special Services. They considered her to have been drugged by me. Plus no one had ever taken someone on a TDU-trip against their will before. She was escorted down a gleaming green hall and that was the last I would see of her.

I was brought to the department of Time Crimes and remanded to a cell of sorts, really just a nice open space surrounded by red lasers that I was warned not to contact. After a few hours my court-appointed council Jake Desbiens arrived. Jake Desbiens said I'd be going down hard, and my best angle would be to balance a hearty amount of contrition with blaming Sam1 at every turn.

"They want to see you take responsibility," he said, "But if you take too much responsibility you'll never get out of the special place in hell they've been designing for you."

"I'm hearing more than I'd like about this so-called special place in hell," I said.

"That's just branding. This government favours punishments that fit the crime. Gone are the days of meaningless incarceration, lifting weights, eating soy loaf, and the other stupidities of your era's prison systems."

"Any idea what my special hell is going to be? It's not going to be like my skin getting peeled off is it? Flaying?"

"I've heard some scuttlebutt involving memory, constant recollection type thing. And when you're not recollecting, you'll be ruminating."

"That doesn't sound so bad," I said.

One of the basic human rights afforded to time criminals brought to consequence in 2061 was an opportunity to catch up on the passage of history. I was given an Internet headpiece that looked like a pair of sunglasses and a quick tutorial on how to use it.

In the almanacs written for TTs coming from the past I encountered an editorial bent downright hostile to my 2016 worldview.

Man-made climate change turned out to be a lot of hot air after all, as temperatures levelled out nicely and no land masses were submerged. The ice caps grew. If anything it got unpleasantly cold for a decade or so, but then that too proved cyclical. Advances in technology allowed crops to thrive; the world enjoyed a golden age of verdancy. Al Gore's estate offered no apology during this period of temperate abundance. I looked up the legacy accounts of the more assured environmentalists I'd known on Facebook, scrolling back years on their walls in search of mea culpas, but found none.

Nick Bostrom's theory that reality was in fact a simulation was concretely proven at Princeton. This finding presented no dramatic change to the human experience, and the watershed realization was soon taken for granted and ignored. It did have a negative influence on church attendance at first, until the major religions reinterpreted their texts to acknowledge the Godhead as some kind of holy game designer. Later a bunch of game design-centric sects and cults emerged, and soon people began to roll their eyes when someone spoke of the Game Designer just as people in my time had rolled their eyes when someone spoke of God.

All the alien stuff turned out to be true, and the disclosure that UFOlogists had long sought came in 2041. This was shortly after the simulation revelation, so by then it didn't even seem to matter. We were characters in a video game, and there were some other characters with different skill sets, but they didn't interact with us on all that overt a level, so so what, you know? Again I looked for apologies from all the smarmy media types who'd rolled their eyes when reporting on extraterrestrial encounters but found none.

For my first meal I was served a dish of aesthetically-displeasing future paste.

"What is this?" I asked the guard.

I say guard, but it was really just some guy in jeans and a t-shirt. The future was very casual.

"Whatever you want," he said, "Close your eyes, picture

what you want it to be in your mind. The nanaprocessors in the food do the rest."

"What about consistency and structure? How do I experience it as a chicken wing if it's mush? I'm not seeing any nub to hang onto."

"Spoon some into your mouth and think of biting into a chicken's wing."

I did. It was like a mouthful of succulent wing meat.

My trial was in the morning. The honourable John D. Wells presided over my trial. Jake Desbiens entered the guilty plea we'd agreed upon, and summarized how I'd been influenced by the irresponsible actions of Sam1, and that since I Sam2 had undergone no time travel training, I shouldn't be held to a high standard of conduct.

Then came the evidence against me. Articles by Brent Steiner were projected on the ceiling and walls of the stupid Time Court. One had a picture of Dave Reid's dad weeping outside the L-S-C courthouse in 2002. Others detailed the funeral of Dave Reid and the town's Reeder-related grief. A sports story by L-S-C Courier sports scribe Will Capulet described the death in terms of the blow to the St. Mark's Cougars' playoff hopes.

Coverage of Sam3's trial came next. My slapdash evidence trail hadn't implicated Blinky, and with the police unwilling to come forward about the disappearing van, Sam3 was the number one suspect. He'd attempted to flee, and then eventually told a lurid story of time travel, sticking with it until he was deemed insane and found Not Criminally Responsible, meaning no jail but a six-year period in the loony bin that he never really recovered from.

"These are the highest crimes one can commit against the occupants of a world," boomed the judge, "Before time travel was even considered remotely possible you planted the seed in a young mind, imposing an untenable reality upon him, such that the young person was believed insane by his peers, and then worse, through counselling was forced to accept his own insanity when he was indeed perfectly sane. This type of misconduct is unforgivable, trained or not. How do you justify these actions?"

"I didn't want him to end up sad like I did," I said.

"Oh dear. He felt sad, how early twenty-first century, like the worst thing is to feel a little bit blue. We aren't all entitled to happiness on this earth. I am woefully unhappy. I wake up each morning, view my wife, and wonder just what might be the point of continuing on. But I don't go messing up entire worldlines because of it," said Judge John D. Wells.

"Dave Reid damaged me," I said, "Dave Reid was going to damage him too!"

"You are an idiot, young man," spoke the judge.

An article was then read from the *Toronto Sun* from 2004. It began:

Forensic investigators are stumped as to why two recently discovered corpses have the exact same dentition...

The head found in the rooming house had been caved in by a cinder block. You better believe dentition is required to identify a person after a cinder block head-caving. Kind of a dark irony that Sam1 succumbed to a stone-based cranial crushing even after I'd spared him.

Teeth were all that survived a self-inflicted shotgun blast to the head of a much younger man found in Grange Park.

Investigators were baffled when both sets of teeth were the exact same, with a 0.000005 margin of error. The only difference being the older man had undergone greater erosion from a longer life of bruxism.

It was all so much so fast that I didn't have the emotional wherewithal to grieve for Sam1, the man who'd become like a brother to me, or for the younger Sam4, so full of promise, whom I'd robbed of a future.

"Here your actions resulted in the death of at least one innocent, Samuel McQuiggan4. And while death was too damned easy a way out for the lecher Samuel McQuiggan1, that too is on your bill, young sir. In addition, you confounded all these poor investigators, shaking their rational-material worldviews to the core. At least one of these investigators quit his job and joined some kind of ashram. I really mean that, an ashram," said the judge.

Some ashram-related tittering from those in the court's pews.

"I'm sorry," I said, "How could I have foreseen all this?"

"It's not that we expected you to know these specific things would happen, but only to heed some basic measure of caution."

The issue of Bethany was raised, but since her reassimilation into her worldline was not yet complete I couldn't yet be held to the fire on that account. An image of Randy looking glum on my original worldline was shown. It lacked affect and the court quickly moved on. This was a sad state of affairs. I'm assuming under normal circumstances the vagabond TT's original worldline was just wrought with all kinds of grief-stricken and confounded loves ones.

"That concludes the evidence against Samuel McQuiggan2. Do you have any last words?" asked the judge.

I could only ask for leniency. It wasn't in my best interest to again cite sadness as a mitigating factor. I was sentenced to five hundred years in the hell they'd designed with me in mind. Jake Desbiens had debriefed me on the advances in life-preserving technology, these apparently having come about in the mid-2020s.

After a one-hour recess the designer of my personal hell was brought out to give a hotly-anticipated presentation. Bill Navilgas plugged something the size of a fingernail clipping into the wall. Navilgas had to take great pains to pinch it between his thumb and forefinger. The tiny-USB struck me as an example of design aesthetics run amok.

"Good afternoon, it's so nice to see so many familiar faces here today. My name is Bill Navilgas, head curator for the Office of Time Crimes. Because of the unprecedented aspects of this case I decided to design and implement the personal hell of Mr. Sam McQuiggan myself. Informed by the statements made by Mr. McQuiggan in the preceding trial, my team and I went back to various years on his worldline to collate materials that would be most difficult for him to bare. Once we had collected all the relevant footage I jumped to my parents' lake house in 2031 to edit it together and convert it for Verisimilitudinous In-Brain compatibility. These images, approximately seventy-two hours in all, will be screened night and day on all the surfaces of Mr. McQuiggan's cell. Should he close his eyes, the VIB content will play on internally, and infernally. That is my little joke. But seriously, he will not be able to escape these memories.

"It was challenging work. Filming Sam McQuiggan and Dave Reid when they were young boys was a personal risk for me. Keep in mind this was just after the satanic panic of the 80s, and just before that show *To Catch a Predator*, so L-S-C residents were almost pathologically obsessed with child molestation. Using a telephoto lens I was able to film them from several miles away. The biggest challenge was working the angles, the town of Lac-Sainte-Catherine not having many tall buildings I could film from.

"Footage of Samuel McQuiggan and Bethany present-ed another minor challenge, as most of their more profound moments took place in the privacy of, to use a colloquial term from the period, *random* bedrooms.

"It was a lonely two years of my life, though only a few minutes have passed here and now, but I do believe it was nec-essary to create a punishment that will fit Mr. McQuiggan's crimes. If it pleases the court I have produced a twenty-min-ute trailer of what Mr. McQuiggan will be experiencing for the next five hundred years."

"It does so please the court," said the judge.

The walls and ceiling went bright. A quote came up on all five screen surfaces:

"You can try really hard to get something back but it'll never be exactly the same." – Anne Tyler.

Given all the annals of history at their disposal I thought they could have come up with something better than that.

It opened on an image of Dave Reid and me as toddlers, falling around in some leaves. This wasn't so bad. I could not consciously recall being a toddler. Then came birthday par-ties. The tire swing in the backyard. Our neighbour Shit Fac-tory getting her tongue stuck to a metal mailbox in winter.

Montage ahead to grade eleven and Dave Reid has just gotten his license, and it's one of those rare nights when he's been allowed to borrow his dad's Camaro. We're driving, and it becomes evident from the POV that Bill Navilgas has attached at least two of his micro-cameras on the Camaro's rear-view mirror, and that song *Night Moves* by Bob Segar comes on The Otter. Dave Reid and I are scatting and be-bopping all over Bob Segar's big radio hit.

"Talking Night Moves…" I first sung.

"Talking' bout those talkin' bout those talkin bout those night moves."

"What kinda moves?"

"Night moves."

"And the subject we're discussing is?"

"Night moves."

"Evening moo-ooves."

"Awww no you know we talking about them night moves."

"Mid-afternoon moves?"

"But no I'm afraid we talkin' bout…"

"So then moves of the…"

"Talking 'bout them Night Moves."

"I was talking about just moves, not moves associated with any particular time of… "

"Night Movesaa."

"Little too tall, coulda used a…"

"Night moves…"

"Talking early morning break of dawn type…"

"Oh no we talking 'bout them Night Moves."

"Uh-huh…"

"And we talkin' 'bout?" a question.

And so on.

The exchange after the *Night Moves* routine spoke of the separation to come: I propose a *Night Moves* scat-parody at the St. Mark's Collegiate talent show, and Dave Reid kiboshes it, knowing *Night Moves* joys won't translate external to the confines of his car.

"Okay, enough for now, maybe," I said to the court.

"Mr. McQuiggan this is only a trailer," said the judge. "Please don't interrupt Mr. Navilgas' fine work and please save your cries of anguish until after at least the first month of your punishment."

High school graduation, skinny-dipping with some girls right before leaving for University, a Mallickian aura of fall days during my first year of University, walking to classes and such, this latter revealing Bill Navilgas' true calling as lyric filmmaker rather than meter-outer of daemonic torment.

Then came Bethany. Not very much good footage in Endocrine where we'd first met for obvious reasons related to lighting, but then walking out together in the morning sun. Our youth and its perfection, unknowable then, got to me and I poured a glass of water from the pitcher before me.

I tried to rationalize that the next five hundred years might not be so bad. Who could know if maybe heaven itself was not just an anthology of a man's finest visions? My trying failed. I knew better. The truest pain, the truest horror, could only come from spent-up grace gone rotten.

Bethany and I kissing in a sun-drenched bed; I guess this representing the high water mark of my life, because then a big discordant cymbal strikes and I see the plates smashing down. I see myself rolling around drunk on some floor. I see myself stumbling around in search of crack. I hear a big drunken monologue of mine that Bill Navilgas lets breathe for a solid three minutes. It had always been my nightmare that someone might film one of my awful scenes. Here it was. Forever and ever.

The trailer closed with the achingly maudlin *David Bowie (I love You Since I was Six)* by The Brian Jonestown Massacre. I had always loved that song, and despite circumstances I was glad to see it had been canonized by a future generation of sentimentalists. I was less pleased that I'd be hearing it in connection with the saddest memories of my life for time inconceivable.

The trailer concluded and the few dozen or so observers in the court burst into a standing ovation for Bill Navilgas' work.

"Bravo," cried one Bill Navilgas fan.

"Fuck all of you sick time dickweeds," I shouted, momentarily sullying the celebratory atmosphere greeting Bill Navilgas' big masterpiece.

A bailiff took me to a holding cell. There a medical man of some stripe came in and outfitted me for a VIB skull port, basically a hole in my skull that a VIB USB key would go in.

I was surprised to find my accommodations quite comfy, with a leather sofa and a Queen-sized bed. A bowl of white mush awaited me on an Ikea dining table. I feared it would taste like mush, but even when I didn't imagine it tasting like anything, it tasted exactly like an Upstairs Bar wing. A few hours later I decided to bite into a buttery lobster roll. Nothing doing. It was another Upstairs Bar wing. Navilgas wanted to leave no sense unfettered by the trappings of the past. The signature flavour of the Upstairs Bar wing, Frank's Red Hot sauce mixed with honey garlic, would be the only taste I'd know for the duration of my internment. Navilgas must have sampled a UB wing or two, and maybe sent one forward in time for the mush producers to use as a prototype. They'd missed the mark on the punishing aftertaste though. After you'd walked down the two flights of stairs and returned to street level it always felt like your mouth had been laminated in stale oil. So really, this was something of a boon to me. If there was a food I might never grow sick of, it was wings. As a young busboy I'd eaten wings every day for the six months I worked at a sports bar in The Central Mall. To me there was no bad wing. A microwaved wing like the ones Pizza Nova foisted on Sam4 and me, a wing sitting under a heat lamp for five hours at a convenience store—that skin-to-meat ratio, that succulence you just won't find on other parts of the chicken, I digress.

I sat down on my couch, crossed my leg, and waited. Another medical man came in and asked if I was ready for the USB key.

"What will stop me from taking it out?" I asked.

"Here we're dealing with a custom punitive model. She'll be removed only by someone with the authorization codes. Those will be passed down through the generations should I choose to die," he said.

I decided to fight him off. The jailers of 2061 enjoyed powers so total they'd grown unaccustomed to resistant outburst. Three or four functionaries were screamed for by the panicked medical man. These fellows lacked any of your 2016-era straps, spit-masks or etc., being armed only with fists, elbows and knees.

"Really now, Mr. McQuiggan," cried the lead medical man, vexed after I'd dug a thumb in his eye. "Really this is beyond being uncalled for. Well past."

Five minutes of thumbing eyes and kneeing groins left me out of gas. As I relented, the USB with its hell was fit into my head slot; that thing then drew me into a world of memories, a world of sadness and nostalgic ache, a world of Bethany's beauty contrasted cruelly against a whole lot of my own asshole behaviour, a world that I would not emerge from for exactly 329.3 years.

28

I had to hand it to Bill Navilgas. The VIB-experience

really captured the essence of my life. As essences go it was not all that chaste, virtuous or upstanding. Navilgas' great strength was to contrast my early innocence (a big smile full of tiny teeth, a hyperactive's giggle) with the desultory wreck of a human being I had gone on to become.

The trailer could never have prepared me for Navilgas' curatorial bravura. He starts the whole immersive shebang off with a solid minute of Lynchian drone, and has obviously instructed his sound engineer to jack the 'sinister' knob on his futuristic version of VIB Pro-Tools all the way up.

In breaks the light. The blinding white of God. The optic benevolence of the aforementioned Terrence Mallick. I am at my first major league baseball game eating nachos and cheese. I'm finally at the Skydome I've only seen on the television in my dank L-S-C basement. They throw the ball so hard, even while warming up. The umpire talks to the first base coach between batters, just two guys doing their job. All kinds of Jumbotron hijinx. Then more drone, and I am at my last baseball game, a disengaged thirty-year-old scrolling through Twitter and Facebook feeds on my phone. By that point I could barely make it down five times a year despite owning a season's pass, yet it's this last ballgame that invokes the worst nostalgia, kind of like how the last episode of *Cheers* is far from the best episode of *Cheers* but still a real heartbreaker.

Navilgas is not above a little low-brow comic relief. Consider my first time masturbating and the little dew drop of semen that makes it out, soundtracked in a clichéd but still hilarious fashion by *Also Sprach Zarathustra*.

He's best in this John Hughes mould. A favourite scene involves an afternoon spent at my buddy B.J. Coeffe's house in the ninth grade, just as I was regaining social acceptance after the perceived theatrical homosexuality scare. B.J. Coeffe's sister was sixteen at the time, wearing very short shorts, a halter top, and scrubbing their father's speed boat. She had the soapy bucket straight out of the 80s Sex Comedy Script-writing Guide for Dummies. She even resembled busty 80s pop sensation Samantha Fox. I am so lured towards this sight that B.J. Coeffe grabs me by the arm and pulls me away from the boat and the suds. Then the moment of comic genius: Navilgas, stationed behind a fence or something, catches B.J. Coeffe quickly looking back at his sister's bod, and freezes on that face for about six beats, a droll encapsulation of the troubled relationship B.J. Coeffe had with his sister's breasts.

Picture every pretty girl you've ever flirted with in your life, with about five seconds devoted to each exchange. And all the funniest jokes you ever told. Picture a long montage of yourself sitting in front of a computer, day after day, different outfits, slumped over at times, very occasionally laughing, all shot on the webcam you'd always meant to but never did put a piece of tape over. Here's Navilgas' most troubling thesis: look at all these things you did Sam, you sat in hot tubs, you witnessed B.J. Coeffe's incestual quandary, you woke up dry-mouthed yet happy on a musty futon with Bethany's legs draped over your thighs. And yet for a third of your life you only sat in front of a computer like a goddamn fool. Immediately following this montage Navilgas interrupts my historical self-referencing with an equally long montage of the many marvels of the world: waterfalls, rainforests, etc. Then there's a cut to me, looking down at a spilled bottle of Corona at Filmore's Gentlemen's Club, and saying, "What a waste."

···· 29 ····

I got to be on friendly terms with the guards. They had a little monitor that showed what I'd be experiencing at any given time, so they wouldn't bring my mush when the on-screen/in-mind me was having sex with Bethany, or at times when I was lying in a stairwell with pants pissed, etc.

Sometimes the guards would tell me about the outside world, and around 2343 I began hearing talk of increasing global and domestic instability. In America there was strife between those living in the big cities, engaging in Time Commerce and generally setting the rules for society, and those living in the agrarian sectors, providing all the soy needed for electronic mush while receiving not that much in the way of recompense.

Given the apocalyptic tenor of my original 2016, it was hard to believe the big nuclear fuck party didn't occur until 2358. Why did America remain safe? Why were the guards and I doing just fine in New New York? Turns out that that allegedly unimplemented Star Wars program had been a go all along, black budgets, shadow gov't as described by Richard Dolan, and all that. You can imagine Sino-Euro-Russian chagrin after their initial acts of nuclear aggression were ineffective. U.S. retaliation was automatic and decisive. Even with the SIDS, even without bothering to use it as a deterrent, the U.S. had the temerity to keep the good old fail-safe system in place, out of spite more than anything, like "How dare you even consider…" which meant the swift end of the aggressors, and the end of just about everyone else for good measure.

The threat to U.S. order then became internal. The guards told me of terrorist attacks and of threats to the supply chain. Then one day no guards came in. Fortunately, the mush had been set to arrive automatically by some concerned party. For forty-five years I knew no human contact, only the sun-drenched or else night-dark images of myself and the images of the others I'd known.

There were weeks, months even, when I was able to convince myself that I enjoyed it, that it wasn't so bad. The images of beauty were still pleasant to behold. I rationalized that the ugly images only served to imbue the beautiful ones with meaning. This was strictly a coping mechanism. More often I prayed for death. Yet I went on eating my mush, filled with life-sustaining, age-preventative technology as it was. There were no tools for suicide available, and you try hunger-striking until death, especially with no one around to prove a point to. The longest I lasted was three days. I don't believe it's humanly possible to starve yourself to death when readily-available mush can taste like the wings of your adolescence, and the water could taste like the finest wine, lime'd Corona, scotch-and-soda, or good Guinness beer, though it could not get you drunk, so I mostly intended for it to taste like green Powerade.

One day not unlike any other, a soccer game in which I'd scored a rare goal playing on screen and in-mind, my solitude was breached. A man with flowing bright white hair and an even whiter robe entered my cell.

"My son, we have waited so many years for this day," he said.

"You have?"

"I am Benevolent Overseer Eldritch. Praise the creator, we have overthrown the tyrannical regime that has imprisoned you here. You will now be free."

"What were you up to for the last fifty years?"

He introduced his all-purpose engineer/tech-guy/right-hand man Burt Arcadian.

"Burt Arcadian is going to remove your VIB input now. That is if you're ready?"

"No time like the present," I said, which I intended as a time travel joke, but years of isolation had dulled my sense of humour and I'm not sure it even registered as a joke. Certainly the Benevolent Overseer Eldritch and Burt Arcadian did not laugh.

"I have some old-time Valium here," said Burt, "Why don't you take it first. The withdrawal after this much VIB exposure...well, no one has ever been so long exposed."

I chewed up two Valiums and felt that immediate benzo relief.

"Get this thing out of me," I said.

He did. I closed my eyes, and experienced indescribable bliss at the long-forgotten non-sight of blackness.

Eldritch briefed me on how the rural militias had won the war against the big city operators of time by cutting off the food supply. When the armies from the city stormed the Woodstocks and the Topekas they found unexpectedly determined forces. The rural areas had antiquated but effective TDUs, making the time aspect of war a stalemate, albeit a messy one. The city folk didn't dare nuke their own bread baskets, knowing they couldn't grow crops in the concrete hell of my parents' generation's construction. The war required traditional ground tactics, but traditional ground tactics were about three-hundred years out of style by then, so a bunch of farm boys with shotguns won a long battle of attrition.

"We have returned to the old way of being, the ways of the ancestors, the approximate year of 1900 being a cornerstone for our mentality. From our research we feel that's when everything started going wrong. I have an offer to make you

Mr. McQuiggan, but first I must ask if there's anything you'd like to do," said Eldritch.

"There is, in fact," I said, "I would like to masturbate to Internet pornography."

"I must say," said Eldritch, "That I find this request rather unwholesome. I'd have thought maybe you'd like to hear a symphony or bite into a crisp apple. But I must remind myself that you come from a poisoned era, and should this be your need I will not stand in the way. Technology is usually limited to the Council of Benevolent Overseers and a few trusted engineers like Burt Arcadian. Given the tumult of your recent centuries I think an exception can be made."

Eldritch cleared his throat and made some eye motions at Arcadian. Arcadian led me to a little office with an old-fashioned HP Laptop.

"Entire Internet is archived here. Just search the name of the website and the year," said Burt.

"Uh, got some tissue or anything?"

Burt Arcadian handed me his monogrammed handkerchief.

"I couldn't," I said.

"I insist," said Burt Arcadian.

I sought out Pornhub 2016 and revelled in debasement for over an hour. Even after I'd finished I continued to watch the filthiest stuff I could find. As Arcadian was leading me back to the office, I asked him, "So you guys really don't watch porn?"

"We enjoy missionary sex for the sole purpose of recreation," he said, appearing like he felt sorry for me.

"Weak," I said.

In the office I detected a certain false cheer from Benevolent Overseer Eldritch. "Ah, glad to see you back and looking refreshed. Now, we have a special surprise for you."

Bill Navilgas was brought into the room by two burly rustics.

"We captured him as a prisoner of war nearly forty years ago," said Eldritch. "This may illustrate that while it took us decades to rescue you, your case was never far from our minds. We have preserved his life with the idea that only you can adequately punish him."

I gave Bill Navilgas an Indian burn of two minutes' duration.

"Why did you do it? Why did you make it such a masterpiece?" I asked.

"I wanted to cement my legacy," he said.

I punched him in the bulb of his nose.

"A good knock!" cried Eldritch.

"No rush," said Burt Arcadian, "But I've been bouncing some ideas around with the other techies. We aren't permitted to go back in time to rob from his life as he did yours, but there's some pretty vicious business we can do to this guy."

I thought it over. I could turn the other cheek. Maybe it would make up for the crummy life I'd led. To hell with it, I thought, my penance had been paid. Back in the little masturbation office Burt and I spent fifteen minutes putting a really heinous VIB-outline together. An intolerable screeching sound would be all that Bill Navilgas would hear again.

"Can you bring up a 4chan gore thread from say 2008?" I asked Burt.

"Here's a five-thousand page archive. Whoa, this stuff is vile," he said.

"Five-thousand sounds like a good number. How about a five-thousand hour montage of all that?" I asked.

Eldritch and I took a car over to the Ritz Carlton. The

workers demining New New York had renovated it to serve as their sleeping quarters. In slumber I dreamt only of the VIB content to which I'd grown so accustomed. This has not ceased to this day. Through free from the VIB-key itself, the work of Bill Navilgas remains a significant part of me, almost all of me in fact.

The next morning, after an actual breakfast of bacon and eggs, Eldritch proposed that I tour the farmlands and tell my story, not unlike those who'd been falsely imprisoned did upon release in my day. It would convince veterans that their war sacrifices were for a greater good, and teach the young about the horrors of the previous regime.

"You might also tell them about your time from 1987, when you became cognizant, to 2016, when you left your worldline. I would ask that you not speak of self-gratification around the children, and please don't have intercourse with any maidens other than for the sole purpose of procreation, and in that case I would hope you were planning on settling down with the maiden in question. I might be able to set you up with a rather pure and beauteous maiden this very day since I'm sensing temptation might be a problem for you from the get-go," said Eldritch.

There went my hopes of establishing some kind of Sam McQuiggan-centred sex cult. Ah, well, these Benevolent Overseers seemed pretty well-entrenched anyway.

"Say, B.O., can I call you B.O.?" I asked.

"After what you've been through, I don't see why not," said B.O.

"I get how the average man doesn't get to use technology or the Internet, but you council guys can mete it out when necessary, right?"

"Yes."

"Does the same go for time travel?"

B.O. paused.

"It does," he said.

"Can you send me back to 2016? My exact worldline. On the day I left. No tomfoolery this time, I promise. I just want to go home."

Eldritch looked disappointed.

"I will not refuse you," he said.

"Thanks man."

In the morning Burt Arcadian showed me to a TDU. He provided info on the logistics around returning to an exact worldline. Normally you couldn't go back to your own past, but my case, like Bethany4's, was an exception because there'd be no original me on that worldline to conflict with.

Burt set the destination for High Park.

Once settled in I said, "Nice knowing you Burt."

"You too Sam. I'll tell my ancestors of you."

"Sure, go for it."

31

And I was back in 2016, just moments after I'd left with Sam1. I stepped out into the February air. Benevolent Overseer Eldritch had outfitted me with a coat and winter boots. He'd also located seventy dollars in antique Canadian money and made a big show of presenting it to me. A cab took me back to my condo. I explained to Marty the front desk guy that I'd lost my keys. Marty let me in. You know what it's like to sleep in your own bed after a long trip?

I nearly forgot about my responsibilities on that worldline. It seemed silly to go into Good Feels after all I'd been through, but then I had nowhere better to be. It was a place to start. Randy sure was excited to see me.

"Not going on trip with father after all?" asked Randy.

"It didn't work out," I said, something of an understatement.

The days passed. No high school figures appeared at Good Feels. I guess John Titor/Chuck must have wrapped things up to some reasonable extent. For that I was grateful.

When ennui or depression struck I struggled not to drink. Though temptation got the better of me on many nights, I'd been through too much just to return for a depressing thirty-year stint of liver destruction leading to a clichéd old Kerouacian death by bloating.

I attended a few AA meetings before determining it was not for me. As tribute to the late Sam1 I began attending Roman Catholic masses instead. The old ladies and the vaguely effeminate clergymen at St. Michael's immediately struck me as the superior support network. If I was going to dedicate myself to a dogmatic system, why not choose one with some grandeur and history behind it? I went to confession and told my whole story. The priest assumed I was crazy, but he listened for almost two hours, which is characteristic of Catholic charity. I figured it would still count as confession in the eyes of God.

Randy started taking business courses at George Brown College during the day. I would edit his assignments for grammar and explain certain idioms from his textbook. A year into his studies he handed me a business plan for a towel-laundering service he planned on pitching to Happy Gilbin, the founder of Good Feels. I read the business plan over. It was sound. Most of the gyms in the GTA didn't have on-site towel washing; they contracted it out. Ours was the exception due to its high towel turnover. Randy needed only $185,000 to buy a used van, rent a space in Brampton for a year, and lease five industrial washers and dryers. He'd done his research on competitors' prices and planned to undercut them by 30%.

"Embarrassment to Happy Gilbin?" he asked.

"Not at all Randy, but I don't think we need Happy Gilbin."

The next day I went to the bank, liquidated my mutual funds and established as much credit as I could. The deal with Randy worked like this: I'd put up the whole $185,000 and once he'd paid me back $92,500 from his share of the profits we'd be equal partners.

He hugged me, and then seemed to regret it. Randy swore he'd do the lion's share of the labour, including driving and washing, while I'd have it easy as the "face of the company to Canada."

Being the face of a towel-laundering company isn't all that onerous. I hustled up clients using Randy's strategy, and within a month we'd stolen a quarter share of the whole towel racket in Toronto. Randy, to the best of my estimation, was working twenty-hour days. If I tried to help I only seemed to get in his way. At the Brampton space I'd see his parents putting loads of towels in. I also suspected they might have been sleeping there at night, based on some fold-up cots I spotted, but I thought it diplomatic not to ask a lot of hard questions.

With all the free time I dedicated myself to good works. All the volunteering in the world wouldn't un-kill Dave Reid3, Sam1, or Sam4, but it made me feel better about myself, and being dead tired at the end of the day made for sleep less haunted by the Navilgas dreams.

While volunteering at the St. Michael's soup kitchen I met Dr. Jessica Rittle, a naturopathic doctor. Healing people by day was apparently not meeting her personal healing quota. She would come in at night and give nutritional advice to the dying bums, offering them B12 shots, sample packs of chewable vitamin C, and all kinds of spiritual aid and succour. She exuded the purest compassion I'd ever encountered. Also, once, when a drunk had groped at her, she'd put him in an arm bar and only relented on the pressure once he'd apologized loud enough for the whole facility to hear. The hobos had given her a standing ovation then, and I can attest that that drunken guy has not lived the incident down among his peer group.

She was only five feet tall, with calves of absurd musculature, for she ran several kilometres per day. She also washed her hair infrequently, no more than once a week, yet somehow it always looked fantastic. She had a small button nose and a pugnacity perhaps born out of being short but brilliant. Dr. Jessica Rittle was well out of my league, but I guess I was able to make her laugh or something, because when I asked her to get coffee one night she accepted, although she did not drink coffee, and neither did I, so we ended up eating bad salads in Fran's Diner.

That night I went home feeling more energized than I had in three-hundred-and-eighty years. I performed one-thousand pushups, not in a row or anything, but still this caused some irreparable tendon damage that I struggle with to this day. I also got a haircut the next morning and started reading *The Encyclopaedia of Naturopathic Medicine* so that I might appear learned in her company.

After a month we were dating, and after a couple incidents far more embarrassing than the Nicole4 debacle she prescribed me a mixture of herbs that alleviated my impotence. I started running with her, and found myself in the best shape of my life.

Amidst all this bliss the Navilgas dreams haunted me, and I'd wake screaming and sweating even in the safety of her giant brass bed. She would ask what was wrong and I wouldn't answer. She would ask who Navilgas was and I would change the subject. Finally she told me if I didn't open up with her then she couldn't continue the relationship.

Naturopathy, though frequently and snidely denigrated in scientifically-dogmatic circles, really does take an admirable approach to the whole *holistic* concept, which word itself has come to represent something of an ugly shibboleth. Dr. Jessica could sound like a neuroscientist when talking neurotransmitters and like Proust himself when talking sad memories. She was also fairly open minded regarding the Fortean, as we often listened to *Coast to Coast AM* before going to sleep.

I decided to entrust my story to her. She concluded that if it wasn't true, that it was so rich a delusion unaccompanied by no other symptoms that even then it was a medical marvel worthy of rigorous treatment and study. She said it would be easiest if she acted like she believed the story. She did not say she believed it, only that she would act that way. Dr. Jessica began to act as my ersatz therapist in addition to being my girlfriend. I'm sure a lot of medical professionals would consider this a terrible idea, and maybe point to the Lars Von Trier movie *Anti-Christ* as an example of all that could go wrong, but over time Jessica began to heal me. I told her of the Dave Reid sadness, of the Bethany regrets, and of my murderous sins of omission.

On a trip to Austin, Texas, where she was attending a conference, I decided to propose. I put two month's towel profits into a ring, even though we both knew that the diamond market was just a sham perpetrated by the DeBeers mining corporation. She said yes.

The wedding would be held at Randy's Mississauga McMansion. There was no question that Randy would be the best man. But after Randy there was an embarrassing shortage of groomsmen for me. Dr. Jessica and I talked it out one night. I had quit drinking entirely, owing largely to her prescription of the nootropic supplements picamilon, ashwaganda, bacopa, tianeptine, and l-theanine. Believe me, I'd told general practitioners of my alcoholic woes and they'd never suggested anything so valuable. She was drinking a glass of wine. We were listening to a late-period Bob Dylan album. The line, "You can't repeat the past, what do you mean you can't, of course you can" was growled by Bob.

"Do you want to reach out to Bethany?" asked Dr. Jessica.

"It would be weird," I said.

"Yeah," she said.

"What about Dave Reid? I think that would be a positive thing for you to do. There is a real Dave Reid after all. Not the guy who showed up at the gym with Bethany. Not the one Navilgas inflicted on you. Not the kid who died. The real guy. The one you grew up with."

We looked him up on Facebook. He was living in Oshawa, owning and operating a Play It Again Sports. I was leery of bringing up too many mawkish friendship grievances. She suggested I approach him as a fellow businessman. I added him to Facebook. Five minutes later I was notified that he'd accepted the Friend Request. Dr. Jessica massaged my shoulders. She asked me if I wanted an L-Tyrosine capsule to aid in dopamine production. We each took an L-Tyrosine capsule.

"Hey man, it's been a while. I see you're a business owner too," I typed, "How have you been?"

Dave Reid is typing…said Facebook, itself a sad and terrible memory machine.

Mike Sauve has written for *The National Post, Variety,* and *McSweeney's.* Previous Montag Press novels include *The Apocalypse of Lloyd* and *The Wraith of Skrellman.* His non-fiction book *Who Authored the John Titor Legend?* also addresses the issue of time travel.

9 781940 233512